The Whole Kitt & Caboodle

A PAINLESS JOURNEY
TO INVESTMENT ENLIGHTENMENT

by

SUSAN LAUBACH

BALTIMORE, MD

Published by Bancroft Press,
P.O. Box 65360, Baltimore, MD 21209
800-637-7377
www.bancroftpress.com

ISBN 0-9631246-1-7
Printed in the United States of America

Designed by Melinda Russell Design, Baltimore, Maryland
Composed in Minion

Second Printing — 1997

3 5 7 9 10 8 6 4 2

For my children and their children, that they may be financially healthy, wealthy, and wise:

Sally, Nelson, Trevor, Susan and Betsy.
Joe, Kit, Emma, Annie and Jack.

ACKNOWLEDGMENTS

Acknowledgments? Where do I start? There has been so much help from so many. My husband Bob supplied the necessary encouragement, reading each draft for me and laughing in just the right places. So did friend and librarian Linda Knox. Tom Emory also contributed his special expertise as a former journalist AND stockbroker and dear friend.

Acknowledgments must also include: Bob Killebrew, from whom I learned so much about money management over the years; Dorsey Yearley, whose integrity and intelligence I observed and absorbed because I was fortunate enough to sit next to him during my first years as a stockbroker; and Jim Price, who can put a complicated financial concept into an understandable story with ease and honesty. These men, among the finest gentlemen and scholars the investment business has to offer, were my teachers and mentors over the (now) nearly twenty years since I, like Kitt, entered the investment world as a financial neophyte. I'll never be able to thank them enough for their contribution to my investment education, which led to the writing of this book.

And, finally, I acknowledge with thanks my dear daughter Betsy Brennen who, with her husband Bob, named our first little granddaughter "Kit," thus beginning this tale in my head; editor and publisher Bruce Bortz, who appreciated that story, guided me through its development, and saw it to fruition; Barbara Jacobs, who suggested that I write this book in the first place; and Mary Park, who put me in touch with Bancroft Press.

By the way, all the characters in this book are fictional, and live only in my imagination (and I hope yours).

CONTENTS

INTRODUCTION

After one of my classes at Chautauqua a few years ago, a student, who's a clinical social worker and former interior designer, said to me, "Why don't you put all this stuff in a book?"

"It's already in books," I replied, pointing to the two I had recommended for the class.

"Not like you tell it," she said. "Those are okay, but they're so boring. I like your stories much better. I learn without realizing it."

"Me, too," said another student, a physician who wanted to manage his own portfolio of stocks in retirement.

"I agree," said another who'd just sold his business and was left holding a huge lump of money for investment.

"In fact, I've been so investment-learning-averse," said the social worker, "that I've avoided taking investment courses for years. My husband made me sign up for this one because he didn't want to do it." She laughed. "Now he's registered for your next class. I told him it's painless. You really ought to put it all in a book," she repeated.

Well, I had actually tried for years to "put it all in a book," but kept turning out these lecture-mode drafts that were even more boring than the ones already published.

Each of these Chautauquans — sophisticated, highly-educated, lifelong learners — convinced me: there *was* a need for a storybook on investments, one that didn't bore them with lectures and jargon, but put the things they needed to know into a format they could read without falling out of their chairs in a deep sleep.

So, here it is, as requested. This is the stuff you need to know to keep hungry stockbrokers at bay when they smell your money and sense your innocence. From this book, you'll be armed with the right questions to ask about both investment advice and investment advisers.

And when someone starts spouting off about the P/E, the ROE, and the S&P, you'll be able to spout right back.

Susan Laubach
Baltimore, MD

CHAPTER ONE: OPENING THE DOOR

KITT MEETS CABOODLE & COMPANY

My name is Caroline Crane and I work — have for almost twenty years — as a receptionist/sales support/margin clerk/and wire operator here at the investment banking firm of Kitt & Caboodle. Eight years ago, when we were still Caboodle & Company, Missy Kitt pushed open our heavy, oak-carved front door for the first time and clicked across the marble floor to my desk.

Her voice echoed eerily in the high-ceilinged former S&L where we had (and have) our office. "Where do I apply for a job?" said she.

"What kind of work do you do?" I inquired.

"What kind of work needs doing?" she shot back, amiably. (I liked her then and I like her now.)

"What's your name?" I asked, thinking that such a smart talker would make a good stockbroker and that Mr. C should see her right away.

"Kitt."

"Kitt what?"

She paused. "It's not Kitt-what but what-Kitt."

"Okay. What Kitt?" I asked.

"Missy," she said, "but everyone just calls me Kitt."

Just then Mr. C came out of his office. "Mr. C, this lady wants a job," I told him. "Missy Kitt, this is Mr. Caboodle, president of Caboodle & Company." I quickly continued before he could slide back into his office. "She asked what needs doing around here and I was about to tell her brokering. What do you think?"

Mr. C regarded Missy Kitt thoughtfully for a moment. I knew he was noting her long, narrow frame even though he seemed to be staring her

full in the face.

She was pretty, with short, reddish blonde hair and blue-gray eyes. And she was thin. Mr. C hated fat. He was skinny and he wanted everyone around him to be skinny.

Unfortunately for us, Caboodle & Company was pretty skinny, too. At least, our part of it. We had lost all eight of our brokers to the new office of a national firm that had opened up in our town the previous month. We were down to me and Mr. C — not what you would call a formidable team.

I watched Mr. C make a couple of quick decisions in his head. You can do that with him: thoughts flit across his face like shadows. It's like flipping through a magazine to watch him think. And I knew just which article he would land on. We desperately needed someone else to sell stocks and bonds at Caboodle & Company. Someone who would work on commission. Actually, someone who would work. Mr. C wasn't too good at that.

After a few seconds of this intense concentration, he thrust out his hand, gave her his big toothy smile and said, "Well, howdyado? What, if anything, do you know about brokering, Missy Kitt?"

"Just Kitt, please. No one calls me Missy." She took his hand and pumped it enthusiastically. "And I know next to nothing — no, make that *nothing* about brokering. But it seems to me that the opportunity for a Kitt to work with a Caboodle is just too good to pass up."

She smiled for the first time and it was like the sun had come up. I had never seen such a smile, like she was lit from within. "Whaddya say?" she asked the now-befuddled Caboodle.

"Say?" he repeated. "As long as you are willing to learn this business and work hard … I guess I say you're hired!"

Kitt cried, "YES!" with delight. She grabbed his hand and shook it some more. Then she turned to me — I was still transfixed by her sunshine smile — and did the same.

"Sign her up, Mrs. Crane, before she changes her mind," Mr.C said, backing into his office and shutting the door.

I smiled back at her and said, "I hope you keep smiling when I tell you about your paycheck, Missy Kitt."

The light dimmed on her face. "I forgot to ask about that."

"Well, brokers work on commission," I said. "We'll pay you a little something while you get trained. After four months, you take your Series 7 test and we'll give you another couple of months to get up and running. Then you're on your own."

I didn't want to be too discouraging, so I continued, "But the work is always interesting, people need to know what you can tell them, and it's possible to make a lot of money. Still want the job?"

She paused for only a moment, then said, "Sounds good."

Kitt Studies to Become a Broker

So Missy Kitt (from Backhoe, Nebraska where her daddy had a farm, she told me) came to work for Caboodle & Company. "I think I can really help my folks, Caroline," she told me right after she was hired. "Dad inherited some stuff from my grandfather and has all these investments in a safe deposit box at the Backhoe Bank. None of us knows what to do with them."

I told her that I had worked for Caboodle & Company for most of my adult life and didn't know much more about stocks and bonds than I did when I came. "Well," I amended, "I know a lot about how this company works and how stocks and bonds get bought and sold. Because a receptionist/sales support/margin clerk/wire operator does just about all the behind-the-scenes stuff that needs to be done when brokers are buying and selling those things."

But the real mystery for me had always been how they make anyone any money.

"So maybe I can help you, too!" Kitt said with what I would learn was characteristic enthusiasm.

All this pent-up demand gave Kitt incentive to start her broker-education with a vengeance. For the first four months, she studied for the required Series 7 at a desk that Mr. C had found in the basement of the old S&L and moved to the big front room where I sat. I would watch her reading the pages of the prep course and could tell the time of day by how near her face came to the book. By one o'clock, her head would begin to bob, and by one-thirty, she was sound asleep, her face resting

comfortably on the cool pages. I wasn't worried by this. I knew Mr. C was sacked out in *his* office at the same time. And God knows, the phone wasn't going to wake them. (It rang so seldom that I'd pick it up now and then just to make sure there was still a dial tone.) Usually around two o'clock, Kitt would wake up, embarrassed.

"Did I snore?" she would sometimes ask.

"Yup. Drooled, too. And I think I heard you grind your teeth," I would invariably reply.

"This is the most boring thing I have ever done," she told me once during her training months.

"It'll be over soon and then the fun begins," I assured her. That was usually enough to get her back to the book again, making a gallant effort to absorb the Federal Reserve System, the Blue Sky Securities Laws, the various Investment Acts of 1933, 1934, and 1940, financial statements, and options strategies.

Eventually it was time for her to take the Series 7, the six-hour exam that the NASD (National Association of Securities Dealers) gives to all wannabe brokers in order for them to be registered with the Securities and Exchange Commission (SEC), the NASD, and the various stock exchanges.

"I remember well the day I took my Series 7," Mr. C said the morning Kitt was scheduled to report to the local testing site.

"When was that?" Kitt asked him.

"November 8, 1965. Of course, I forgot it all by November 9, 1965. We took one of those crash courses in New York and then had to go down to one of the NYU classrooms to take the test. We wrote it all out — paper and pencil," he said, in wonder, like he had hewn the exam out of stone or written it in cuneiform or something. Kitt would take her Series 7 on a computer, touching the screen to give her answers. When finished, she'd find out on the spot if she'd passed.

And, of course, she did. Kitt had practically memorized the study material. "You'll do well on commission," I told her later, when she reported her test results with great relief. "Your anxiety level is high enough."

"Is that what it takes, high anxiety?" she asked.

"Certainly helps. Think of the commission report as your report card and I'll bet you'll make sure you get all A's." I knew girls like Kitt in school. C's made them crazy.

Kitt Begins Her New Career

Kitt began her assault on potential customers the day after she took her exam. "I'm going through the Yellow Pages and calling all the accountants," she announced. Sure enough, that's what she did. First, she called them. Then, she went to see them. Pretty soon, she was asking me how to fill out new accounts forms so that she could buy stocks for the first of her new clients.

After accountants, it was acupuncturists, then associations, automobile dealers, bail bondsmen, barbers, and beauty salon owners. She was up to building contractors by Spring. Anyone who would sit still long enough for her to introduce herself was treated to that smile and her rapid-fire pitch on Caboodle & Company, its research, and her interest in helping them make money.

Luckily, even though we had lost our retail stockbrokers in the sweep by National (they cleaned out a lot of other local firms, too), we still had some good research analysts left. These guys did good work checking out the companies with whom our other departments — Corporate Finance, Mergers and Acquisitions, Institutional Sales, and Trading — did business.

I hardly ever saw Kitt in those early days. She'd come in very early and read all the research that had come in overnight from the services we got by subscription. Then she'd read the *Wall Street Journal* and the *Investors' Business Daily* and *The New York Times*, all the time making notes, cutting out stuff and putting it in her notebook.

Everyday she'd leave me a long list of things to do: letters to write, tickets (those are the things brokers fill out in order to buy or sell stock) to complete and file, phone calls to make. By the time Mr. C and I had jointly pushed open the old S&L doors to start work in the morning, Kitt would be gone. But, during the day, she'd call in every hour or so to catch up on what was happening.

The woman was a dervish. Neither Mr. C nor I had ever seen such activity in a broker, old or new. Oh, she wasn't doing any really big ticket business. In fact, her commission sheet was full of treasury trades, government agency bonds, stuff like that. No money in those things for the broker, and hardly any for Caboodle & Company either. But she was meeting people. And learning how to talk to them about stocks and bonds.

Once or twice a week, Kitt would make it back to the office before I left for the day. Then she'd sit right down at her desk and start calling whatever group she was working her way through for more appointments.

I wish I could say that this hyperactivity paid off for Kitt. She was doing everything a person could do to make it big in the brokerage business. Prospecting for customers, reading the research, getting out and talking about investments — what more could a person do? But the business didn't come in. No one was buying what Kitt was selling: her skills as a stockbroker. People just didn't seem to believe that Kitt could make them money. As it turned out, neither did she.

Mr. Caboodle

Now and then Mr. C would glance over the pages detailing Kitt's commissions (her so-called commission run) and mutter to himself. There wasn't much he could do for her since he didn't know anything about getting business either. Mr. C hadn't met a customer in years, maybe decades.

Mr. C is what used to be called a "scion" and is now referred to as a member of the Lucky Genes Club. His great grandfather had started Caboodle & Company, having made his pile in the stock market of the previous century. He and his successors managed to avoid the market's various crashes with adroit moves at just the right times. Over the years, the Caboodle fortune had grown to where it was regularly listed in the Forbes 400. Mr. C was an extremely rich man.

Luckily for the fortune and the company, he was also a shy man with simple tastes. His interests ran along the lines of ironing his own shirts

(claims it relaxes him), cooking his gourmet meals, tending his garden (okay, so it's an orchid farm), and driving his chauffeur to and from doctor appointments and the elder care facility. His chauffeur was 86-years-old and was part of Mr. C's inheritance. At his age, Charles needed more tending than either the orchids or the fortune.

Mr. C had never married, although many women with large teeth who looked like they could run in the Preakness had come through our doors, or called him on the phone, speaking in that strange, nasal, wired-jaw accent that must be taught in some School for the Very Rich somewhere. "Tll Mr.Cbdle tht Muffy clld."

Anyway, it was clear to all three of us that Missy Kitt was getting nowhere and that Mr. C was completely unable to do anything about it.

CHAPTER TWO: LEARNING FROM THE PAST

Kitt Regroups

One day, Kitt came back to the office early. She sat down on the fake leather sofa and looked at me with large, sad eyes. "I just figured something out, Caroline," she said. "I don't *know* anything."

"Huh?" I replied.

"I read all this research and meet all these people and babble on about stocks and bonds and money market funds and *I DON'T HAVE A CLUE WHAT I'M TALKING ABOUT.* I'm not fit for this business at all!"

"Of course you are!" I said. "You're as good a broker as anyone!"

She smiled weakly. "No, but I *am* broker than I was. Ha. Ha. I can't even pay my rent this month. And I sure don't want to write home for money when they're waiting for me to do magic with Grandpa's Portfolio."

"Kitt," I began firmly, "you passed your Series 7 with nearly a perfect grade. You know a lot more than you think you do."

"No, I don't. That test doesn't teach you anything about how to make money with investments. It just teaches you about Blue Sky Laws and the Federal Reserve and other stuff that's totally useless."

I had to agree with her there. Naturally, brokers had to learn about Securities Law so they didn't break it (or so they'd know *when* they were going to break it). But stockbrokers never learn in any formal way how to advise people on investing their money, which is what most people think the job is supposed to be. The lucky ones are guided by older, experienced, conscientious brokers who keep the rookies from making too many mistakes. And it really IS luck — who you sit next to, who you become friends with. And the rookie doesn't even KNOW whether the older, experienced guy (there aren't many gals) is conscientious or a

commission-generating con man.

Of course, none of that would help Kitt. She sat next to no one, all our former brokers having skipped to National Investments down the road. And while Mr. C was a broker, it was in name only. He rarely put in a ticket other than for his own account.

But then a thought struck me. It was weird, but it might work. And it might help both of us make some money out of Caboodle & Company.

"Kitt, do you own any stocks or bonds?"

"You mean, other than what Dad inherited in Grandpa's Portfolio? Of course not. You've seen my commission run. You buy stocks and bonds with money, and I'm not making any."

"Well, I think you need to see how this stuff really works. So I've got an idea." She looked at me expectantly. I drew a deep breath and went on. "Okay. Here it is. I've got a little money in CDs." (This certificate of deposit money was residue after the fast-talking former Caboodle & Company broker got through with my savings. Neither he nor I knew what he was doing. Even with Kitt's inexperience, I thought she could do better with my money than he had.)

"You match my contribution with a little of your money. Do you think your Dad would let you raise some money by selling something in Grandpa's Portfolio?"

Kitt nodded slowly. "Maybe. I guess."

I continued. "We'll set up a joint account for you to invest."

"You'd do that?" She was incredulous.

"Yes," I answered firmly. "I need a good, honest broker. We're both probably going to retire in thirty to forty years. We need to start investing now. I know that much. And I also know I'm not making anything in the CDs." This was certainly true. "But," I went on, "there's a catch to this plan. Have you ever been in the storeroom here?"

"No. Why?"

"Because Mr. C has kept ALL of his family's investment records there. Someday, he wants to write a book about the Early Caboodles. He has boxes and boxes of old statements and ledger sheets and personal diaries upstairs in the storeroom."

"Okay. So what?"

"Look. The Caboodles were nothing if not rich. And they got that way from investing. If you go through that stuff and figure out how they did it, you can do the same thing with our money. I'd do it myself but I couldn't really make head or tail out of it. You'll know much better than I would what they were doing and talking about."

Kitt looked at me, dumbstruck. Then the sun started to shine: a smile grew across her face.

"A great idea. That is a really great idea. But won't it take forever to go through?"

"Not really. Mr. C has been organizing it over the years. When he isn't napping, he's in the storeroom."

Kitt Learns How It Was Done By The Caboodles

So Kitt began to spend part of every day studying the investing history of Mr. C's forebears. Dragging box after box from the storeroom into the rickety elevator cage, she would descend from the second floor with her treasure and haul it across the marble floor to her desk. Then she would immerse herself in the yellowing statements and fading ledgers that chronicled the growth of the family fortune.

One day, Kitt looked up at me and said firmly, "I think I'm finally catching on."

"I knew you would."

"It's a lot like trees," she said.

"Huh?"

"Back home in Nebraska, we had trees for only two reasons: they either grew big or they grew fruit. Stocks do the same thing," she said before going back to her reading.

"Say what?" I inquired politely.

To hold her place, she turned down the corner of the page she was reading and set the book down. "Well, think about it. You buy shares of stock in a company because you think that the company is going to grow bigger and so the shares of stock are going to be worth more. Don't you?"

I had to agree with that. "But sometimes you want to get the dividends that the company pays," she went on. "Those companies that pay

big dividends, like utilities, don't usually grow as much, right?" I nodded.

Her voice rose as she warmed to her subject. "Well, the important thing is to know which is which. I mean, for which reason did you buy or do you own each security: For income or for growth?"

She was looking at me so intently that I answered, "You tell me. What are you going to buy for us first: a shade tree or a fruit tree?"

"What do we need at this point in our lives? We don't really need the fruit. I'm not living royally, but I'm finally earning enough to pay my bills."

"Me, too. And I don't want to pay a lot more taxes, which I would have to do if I got more income."

"Right."

"What about mutual funds? Should we buy some of those? That seems to be a good way to go if you don't know what you're doing."

Kitt looked pained. I added quickly, "Not that you don't know what you're doing. I didn't mean …"

"Hey, no problem. We both know the extent of what I know. That's why I'm going through this stuff." She gestured to the pile of Caboodle papers surrounding her. "But I have a feeling that you don't just leap in and buy mutual funds either.

"You have to know something about who's managing them, what kinds of stuff they buy for the fund, how much they cost, how well they've done. There's a lot of …" Her voice trailed off. She looked at her watch and picked up her pencil.

"Let's hold off a bit on our buying. Before we do anything, I'm going to start making a list of investment rules so that I can keep this Caboodle stuff straight." Kitt leaned over her memo pad and wrote down the first of what became her rules, her commandments.

KITT & CABOODLE'S COMMANDMENTS

1. Know why you own each security:
for income (money you need now) or for growth
(money you'll need later).

"Of course," she mused, "sometimes you can be real lucky. You'll buy a shade tree and eventually get fruit, too. I remember a cherry tree back home that was three stories tall. And look at some of the stuff these Caboodles bought. At first, there were tiny little dividends or none at all. But the companies raised the dividends every year and now they're pretty big compared to what the Caboodles paid for the stock all those years ago."

"Good reason to hang on to stock instead of selling it, right?" I asked.

"Sure. Unless something terrible happens to the company, like what happened to Continental Shirtsleeves in the early 80's."

Kitt grabbed a fistful of papers and pulled a customer statement. "See here?" she pointed to an entry. "Caboodle Sr. sold it in July. That was just after the company said it was going to expand into the auto parts business."

She pulled out another piece of paper, a list. "You can see right here: The old guy wrote down reasons for owning everything. In the late 70's, he bought Continental because of expansion in the shirtsleeve industry, so naturally he sold it when it looked like they were going in an entirely different direction. Voila!

"And here's another." She pointed to an entry in one of the journals. "Here's this little day care company, a perfect thing to buy with so many women going to work in the early 80's. Caboodle writes: 'Visionary Mgt. Leader in niche mkt. 20 yrs. daycare biz. Pure play.' All his reasons to buy Dippety Day Care stock."

"Excuse me, Miss, but what's 'pure play'?"

"It means the company didn't do anything else. If you wanted to play" — she stopped, then continued — "… if you want to *invest* in the day care business, this company was entirely devoted to it: a 'pure play.'" Kitt looked down at the page again. "But then, here …" she ran her finger down the page and read aloud, 'Dippety buys S&L, insurance co. SELL.' And he's out of it. History.

"And he was right to do that. I checked. Dippety went from 14 to 6 over the next few years. They're barely hanging on today." She looked down at what Caboodle had written and then up at me. "No longer 'visionary,' no longer 'leader in niche market.' Certainly not a 'pure play' when they added insurance and banking to their business."

Kitt set the papers down and went on, "So that's another one of our rules. 'Write down the reasons why we bought something and sell when those reasons are no longer valid.' In fact, from what I've read, that is the ONLY time a stock should be sold — when the reasons you bought it are no longer valid."

KITT & CABOODLE'S COMMANDMENTS

2. Write down the reasons you bought each security and sell only *when those reasons are no longer valid.*

Bad Weather in Backhoe

While she was still plumbing the Caboodle investment archives, Kitt carried on an active correspondence with large numbers of hometown folk who wrote her at the office. "They get a kick out of addressing the envelopes," she explained. "You know, 'Missy Kitt, Caboodle & Company.' They think I'm a big deal here," she added sheepishly.

"There's no question you *are* a big deal here, Missy Kitt," I told her firmly. "You are our entire retail division."

One day a letter with the now-familiar Backhoe postmark visibly upset Kitt. "My cousin Harold says the weather has been fierce back home. Daddy lost all his early lettuce and has no spring crop."

She looked up from her desk, her brow wrinkled with worry. "I told him he had to have some other backup crop — lettuce is so fragile. I don't think my dad was cut out to be a farmer."

Suddenly, it was like someone had flipped the overhead light switch onto high beam. Out came the smile.

"You know what old Caboodle would have done, don't you?" she asked me. She went on without waiting for my reply.

"He would have been ready for bad times by doing what Dad *should*

have done. See, the Caboodles set up their investments so that something was always working for them, no matter how bad things were." She rifled through the papers and pulled out one of the yellowing statements. "Like when there was the stock market equivalent of a bad spring." She brandished a paper that I could see was dated October 1974 — a *very* bad "spring."

"These Caboodles were smart," Kitt said with admiration in her voice. "They had money tucked away in Treasury bonds, and" — pulling an old statement from the pile — "some good old Triple A, tax-free municipal bonds. These things paid interest no matter WHAT the stock market was doing."

"And it was doing terrible things. I remember." And I did. That year nothing good was happening. There was so little business that brokers were becoming bus and cab drivers to support themselves. "It was a dreadful stretch," I said.

"Well, not for the Caboodles. They could still rely on the interest from tax-free bonds and treasury bills to get them through. They never had to sell their stock in a panic.

"It's important to own both shade trees and fruit trees, Caroline."

"In other words, Miss Kitt," I added, "diversify."

"You got it," she said.

KITT & CABOODLE'S COMMANDMENTS

3. Don't try to time the market:
Diversify to lower your risk.

MR. C WAKES UP

While Kitt was learning all this stuff about the Caboodles and their investing history — ostensibly so that she could invest the money in our

new joint account — Mr. C was beginning to wake up from his decades-long nap and take a new interest in the business. Kitt's excitement was contagious. He may not have been much of a broker, but Mr. C knew a lot about the investment business. Must have absorbed it by osmosis, in his crib or something.

Kitt took to asking him questions about certain companies. At first, he looked positively dumbfounded. No one had asked him a question about stocks for years.

"Electric Images, Inc? Uh, Electric Images, Inc. ..." Then he would scurry over to the Standard & Poor's books or to the Value Line collection and begin to leaf through them, until he came to the page for the company she was asking about. "Yup! Right here. See for yourself," he would tell her, no doubt proud that he had remembered how to look it up.

Pretty soon, though, he began to bring up other things: things like the company's debt load and whether the earnings were growing or not. It was like waking up a slumbering genius. Mr. C seemed to have a real knack for the financial details about a company and an interest in researching them, once Kitt was there to get him started and to talk to him.

The office, by this time, was beginning to show the effects of Kitt's employment with Caboodle & Company. House plants had replaced the dust in most corners of the front room. Kitt's mother had sent her a homemade rag rug that she placed under the old leather sofa. "It looks great," I told her when she laid it down. "But don't you want it in your apartment?"

"I'm here more than I'm there," she explained.

Life Stories of Good Companies

About this time, Kitt became interested in learning more about individual companies. She was trying hard to find the perfect investment for what she called our "joint portfolio" (which at that time looked more like a coin purse than a portfolio).

"I think it's very important to know where a company is in its life story," she said to me one day, sitting at her desk surrounded by Caboodle

lore.

"Would you like to explain that?" I asked, putting down the tickets I was posting in her account book.

"Sure. This may sound funny, but I think that companies are a lot like people."

"Go on," I urged.

"What you do with them depends on where they are in their life story." She looked pleased with herself.

"Companies or people?" I asked.

"Both. Look at it this way: you have to watch babies every minute or they'll stumble and fall. It's the same with baby companies. They grow really fast. They're interesting because they're into a lot of new things all the time, but there's always this risk that they'll fall down and hurt themselves. Like this little fast-lube company that Caboodle bought just as soon as it went public. See here?" She held out a page from the Caboodle records. "They expanded too fast and it was nearly down the tubes with fast-lube.

"When these little companies get to be teenagers," Kitt continued, "they don't need to be watched all the time, but ..."

"They need to be monitored," I interjected. "Keep them on the straight and narrow ..."

"Right. Teenager-type companies, like this restaurant chain that's been so successful." She held up an annual report that Caboodle had saved in a file with the company's name on it. "And teenager-type people are still exciting, growing pretty quickly, but not as fast as when they were babies."

"That's neat, Kitt," I said, and then thought for a minute. "But what about grownups?"

"Grownups are the blue-chip companies. They've been around forever. You don't have to watch them all the time because what they do is pretty predictable. But they're still growing in their thinking and planning. They're expanding, researching, going into new markets. The grownups just aren't as flashy or as scary as the babies, but they can be very comfortable to be with."

"So what happened to XYZ Foods?" I asked, referring to a firm in our city that had certainly been around forever but wasn't doing any

growing that anyone could notice. In fact, XYZ was shrinking.

"It retired early!" Kitt said triumphantly. "Entered a vegetative state."

"Possibly senility?"

"Right!" she laughed. "So you can see how important it is to know where a company is in its life story."

KITT & CABOODLE'S COMMANDMENTS

4. Know where a company is in its life story in order to understand its risk and reward potential.

The days began to take on a certain rhythm. Mr. C and I would get to the office at around 8:30 every day. Kitt would be gone, but there was evidence everywhere that she'd been there before us: coffee container from Dunkin'Donuts, open newspapers with articles sliced out, long lists of things for me to do, and written-out questions for Mr. C. Come ten or ten-thirty, the phone would ring and it would be Kitt.

"Hi, it's me, Kitt," she'd always begin.

"Hi, Me-Kitt," I would answer. "How's it going?" I'd ask.

And she'd tell me about her appointments.

CHAPTER THREE: HELPING COMPANIES GROW

MOM'S MUMS AND THE VENTURE CAPITALISTS

One day, Kitt told me about Mom's Mums. She had met this woman who raised chrysanthemums, and showed them at the annual Autumn Craft Fair. "They're absolutely the most gorgeous mums I've ever seen," Kitt told me. "She sells the blooms during most of the summer and fall, and then, for Thanksgiving and Christmas, makes and sells these spectacular dried arrangements. Mr. C ought to see them. We should get some for this office."

A week after exchanging business cards with the woman, Kitt called her and made an appointment, just to get to know her better. This was the way Kitt did things then. She'd just go talk, or rather, listen to people talk about their businesses and families and plans for the future.

Kitt showed me Mom's business card, on which was written "Mom's Mums, Mona Malloy, President."

"Her name is Mona but a lot of people do call her Mom. She has six kids. Her business is growing, Caroline." She laughed.

"I mean, besides growing mums and kids, her company is growing, too. People love these flowers. She keeps getting bigger and bigger. All six kids are working there now and they still can't keep up with the demand for Mom's Mums."

Mr. C, who had materialized silently and was thumbing through the "Occupant" mail, looked up and said, "Caboodle invested in Mom a couple of years ago. Good woman, Mona. Smart. Makes good mums." Then he turned and went back into his office.

"Invested in Mom's?" Kitt asked.

"I guess he means through Victory Ventures," I said, referring to the

venture capital group that some crafty Caboodle cousins had formed years ago. Mr. C was part of the group that invested in promising companies early in their business lives.

"Victory puts money into these companies to help them grow. Mom's Mums would be right up Mr. C's alley. He's quite a gardener, you know."

Venture capitalists usually stick to something they know well. Then they can help a company through its growing pains, offering advice about the industry and how to make money in it. Not that Mr. C knew much about the money-making part of it, but his cousins did.

Mom and Kitt became good friends. Kitt found the records on Victory Ventures in the Caboodle papers and read up on the problems that young companies face. She listened as Mom talked about the markets for mums, the difficulties she had in getting distributors, and the high cost of growing the company.

And, of course, being from a farm, Kitt knew about growing things, like mums, in the ground. So she and Mom had a lot to talk about.

When his old friend Mona would come to town to see Kitt, Mr. C began coming out of his office. The three would sit around musing on the relative difficulties posed by mums versus orchids, which Mr. C raised.

Often, the subject would turn to Mom's plans for the future of her company.

Taking Mom's Public: The Initial Public Offering

One day, Mr. C said, "You know, Mona, I think you should consider taking Mom's public." (Oh, goody, I thought. Now we'll buy some stock in a great new *public* company, which is made up of common stock shares that members of the public — like Kitt and I — can buy through one of the stock exchanges or over-the-counter. I'll explain those exchanges later.)

"I know, I know," said Mona. "I need to get some of my money out of the company to pay for the kids' colleges."

"Well, Victory Ventures is probably ready for that, too. Lots more ventures out there to fund. It's been, what? Four, five years now since we first got together with Mom's Mums?"

"At least that. I just hate the thought of — *you* know, it wouldn't be just Mom's Mums then, or even Mom's Mums and Victory Ventures. It'd be Mom's and a couple of million other folks who'd own my company."

"This is true," said Mr. C sympathetically. "But you'd still own the biggest piece. And, of course, you'd still run it the way you want to."

So Mom and Mr. C began talking about selling part of Mom's Mums to the public in an initial public offering of stock.

"You can sell half the company, Mona … say about 55% of a total of six million shares." Mr. C was beginning to sound like an investment banker again.

"How much money would I get out of that, Carl?" Mona was one of the few people who called Mr. C by his first name. Probably because he didn't call her Mom.

"You mean, how would we price the shares? Well, there aren't many companies like yours that are publicly owned. You know, companies that people can buy shares of stock in, so I guess we have to compare Mom's Mums to a specialty retail store like Frankcraft." Frankcraft is a company that sells craft supplies and house plants.

"I just couldn't tell you that right now. I'd be guessing, Mona. We'd have to get the Caboodle corporate finance people to tell you that. They need to put together your past earnings, projected earnings, do the due diligence, that kind of thing."

"Due diligence" is the legal work that has to be done before offering any new stock. Like checking out whether the earnings have grown and where they've come from and who the top management people are and how much of the company they'll own after the initial public offering, which is called an "IPO" for short.

All this legal information goes into the prospectus. This is a booklet that has to be given to people who want to buy the stock BEFORE they can buy it. The law. It doesn't have the offering price in it, because that hasn't been decided yet. So there is red printing along the side of the front page, telling you that this is not the "final." Because of this, the "preliminary" prospectus is also called a "red herring." Don't ask why.

Mr. C took out his little pocket diary and began to leaf through its empty pages. "Let's see. Can we get you together with that team next week?" He looked at her hopefully.

"Okay," Mona answered. "I guess so. Can't hurt to get started talking about it." She gathered up her things and started for the door. Both Kitt and Mr. C rose and walked with her.

No sooner had they seen her out than Kitt turned and said, "Corporate finance people? Who are they?" She looked around as if she expected to find them materializing in the corners of the big front room. "Did you hire more people while I was out on calls?"

Mr. C laughed. "No, Kitt. Caboodle & Company has a corporate finance department that my brother runs. The office is around the corner. They haven't done much since we lost our retail sales team.

"See, when a company gets ready to sell its stock to the public, it likes to know that there are going to be stockbrokers to do that — you know, to take the story to the customers and get them to buy the shares."

"I don't want to throw cold water on this, Mr. C," I interjected. "But you still don't have what one would call a sales team." I looked apologetically at Kitt. "Sorry, Kitt. But even a dervish like you can't do the kind of work required to place an initial public offering. Even with a big syndicate to help you."

Rarely does an investment banking firm get to sell the entire IPO itself. Usually a group of firms, called the "syndicate," distributes the stock to its customers.

Mr. C sat down on the couch. He looked dejectedly at his shoes. "You're right. Why would Mona choose Caboodle & Company. I must be crazy to think she'd give the deal to us."

"Well, Caboodle certainly knows her business better than anyone else," Kitt said. "Doesn't that count for something?"

"I don't know. Those guys at National Investing will be all over her when they hear Mom's might go public. Most of the brokers used to work here, so they'll know her, too."

"Not really," I said. "The retail brokers usually don't know anything about what's happening with Victory Ventures. I'll bet you most of them didn't even know we had a venture capital group. Kitt only found out because she and Mom became friends."

When Caboodle Might Lose the Deal, Kitt Rides to The Rescue

But Mr. C was right. When he called Mom to arrange for her to meet with his brother's group, she told him that her phone had been ringing off the hook with calls from other bankers.

"All of a sudden, I'm extremely popular, Carl," she said. "National is coming here tomorrow, wants to 'get to know me better,' they said. How about *that*?"

"Well, you're right to talk to them," Mr. C said sadly. "They know what they're doing and they certainly have the sales force to place the stock." No one ever faulted Mr. C on his integrity.

Kitt and I overheard this conversation through Mr. C's open office door. We looked at each other in dismay. She had been doing her usual afternoon studying of the Caboodle papers and was surrounded by statements, ledgers, and dusty boxes.

"Darn it, Caroline," she said to me. "I'm not going to sit around and let this thing fall through." She stood up abruptly, ignoring the pile of papers that slid to the floor from her lap. "I've got some phone calls to make."

Kitt had made some friends in the financial community, and called one of them, a fellow named Joe Schmidt who worked at the American Investment Company, a local brokerage firm similar to Caboodle & Company. "Hey, Joe. Can we have lunch today?" she asked. "I need to ask you about something."

She listened to Joe for a minute and then said, "I'll meet you at noon, okay?" and hung up. A minute later, she was speaking to Harry Jones at National.

"Meet me at 1:00, Harry?" After Harry, she dialed another number. "How about having a cup of coffee with me at 2:00, Jack?" Pretty soon, she had the entire afternoon filled with appointments to eat and drink, one-on-one, with the local brokerage community.

"I'm going to find out how the big boys do it, Caroline," she announced, grabbing her purse and heading for the door. "See you later."

I didn't see her until the next morning. She was still at her desk, reading the Caboodle papers and making notes, when Mr. C and I arrived.

"So how'd it go yesterday?" I asked.

Kitt waited until Mr. C had disappeared into his office. "Great. I heard all about things like road shows and institutional investors and how stock gets placed on an offering. And I think we can do it, Caroline." She stood and walked over to my desk, and looked at me earnestly.

"A road show is when the company's management team and investment bankers go to cities where there are big investors, like people who manage billion-dollar pension plans, mutual funds, things like that. The company's president tells these institutional investors (that's what these guys are called when they're that big) why this is a great company and why they should buy its stock.

"These people I talked with yesterday, they tell me that Caboodle & Company used to be pretty well thought of and still has a lot of contacts. And I've got Kitt cousins in just about every major city in the country, not to mention brothers and sisters. I think we could do this, Caroline. I think we could pull off a really good roadshow and sell a lot of Mom's stock." She paused. "And Joe thought so, too," she added.

"You told Joe?" Corporate finance talk is highly hush-hush. "You probably shouldn't have told Joe," I said, trying not to sound upset.

"I trust him. Besides, everybody has heard by now that Mom's is thinking of going public." Kitt leaned over my desk and said in a whisper, "I think Mr. C could get Joe to come to work here, along with a couple of other guys, too. They aren't happy at American."

"But why would they want to come here?" I asked, astounded.

"Why not?" said Kitt. "I told them about the opportunities in a small company like ours, the resurgence of Caboodle & Company as an investment banking firm, the percolating that's going on with Victory Ventures. They got all excited."

So Kitt, while learning about roadshows, had been out recruiting. I had to hand it to the woman. She was indefatigable.

In a few weeks, the sales force at Caboodle & Company was restored to its former grandeur. We now had a team of seasoned brokers plus Kitt, who was like an entire team herself.

Meantime, Mr. C and Kitt made the pitch to Mona. It went something like this: "Caboodle & Company has corporate finance people with plenty of experience to do the due diligence.'"

And (thanks to Kitt) we also had the brokers to distribute the stock. Furthermore, Caboodle & Company was resuscitating its "specialty retailing" analyst to do the research on Mom's Mums, which was in the industry that he (the analyst) knew intimately.

To everyone's delight, Mona agreed that Caboodle & Company would be the investment banking firm to offer Mom's Mums to the public for the first time. There would be a selling group of other companies to help with the offering, but we were to lead it.

Kitt was out of the office for a couple of weeks after that, doing the Mom's Mum's roadshow. The response to the offering was really good. It seemed that a lot of people were gardening enthusiasts, and a lot more were excited about the interior decorating part of the business. There weren't many companies doing what Mom's Mums did. The institutional investors were getting excited.

"That's good and bad, Caroline," Kitt pointed out to me when she called in one day.

"What could be bad?" I asked. (Mr. Caboodle had never fully explained these things to me in all the years I've worked here.)

"There isn't much stock in this initial offering," she replied. "It's only three million shares and there's a lot of demand. Not enough shares to go around."

"That's called 'hot', right?" I asked.

"Yeah, but it makes me nervous. See, if it's really hard to get the shares, it's possible that Mom and Mr. Caboodle will decide to increase the number. I guess Mr. C knows what he's doing, but it seems like printing money to me. Just makes the shares worth less in the long run."

"Couldn't they simply raise the price?"

"That's probably what'll happen. The price range now is between $8 and $10 a share. So it'll probably go up to, say, $12 to $14 a share."

"That ought to make Mom happy," I said.

"It will if people are as excited at twelve to fourteen dollars as they were at eight to ten." Kitt sighed. "It's a fine line, this pricing stuff. If the price shoots way up the first day the stock trades, Mom's going to think we didn't ask enough. If the price drops quickly, the investors are going to be unhappy."

Multiples and Growth Rates

Something had been bugging me for years, something I never really understood about this business. So I decided one day to ask Kitt. "Just how did they come up with the $8 to $10 in the first place?" I inquired.

"Lots of homework. Looking at other companies that do the same kind of thing — in this case, that serve the hobbyist market or the home decorating market. Trying to anticipate how fast Mom's earnings are going to grow and putting a reasonable multiple on that growth."

"What, what, *WHAT*?" She was talking much too fast for me. "What, pray tell, is a 'reasonable multiple?'"

"Oh, gosh, I'm sorry. I'm starting to talk just like Mr. C. The multiple is the result of dividing the stock's price by what the company earned per individual share of stock. It's what people call 'the p-e' or 'the price/earnings ratio.'"

"Well, thanks a lot, that sure explains it all," I said. "Do it again, please?"

"Say Mom's Mums goes for $10 a share. According to the prospectus, the company earned, or profited, about 20 cents a share last year. The people who analyze companies — those guys upstairs in the research department — expect it to earn thirty cents next year. Well, assume the price is $10 and the earnings per share comes to 20 cents. Ten dollars price divided by 20 cents earnings is 50. So, if Mom's shares are priced at ten dollars, then, based on last year's earnings, its multiple is 50."

Ten dollars divided by twenty cents, I repeated to myself. Right, fifty. Okay. "Okay, so far," I said aloud.

"That's a pretty high multiple. But if you do the same thing and use this year's earnings estimate ..."

"Thirty cents a share?" I asked.

"Right. At the price of $10, earning thirty cents a share, the multiple is about 33. Still pretty high, but earnings are growing fast, too — at a 50% rate, between last year and this, if the estimates are correct."

"Wait a minute. What does *that* have to do with it?"

"Well, most of the people who buy this kind of stock — you know, a small, new, and fast growing company — are buying it because it is growing quickly.

Price: $10
Earnings per share (estimate for current year): .20
Price divided by EPS (P/E): 50
EPS (Next year's est.): .30
P/E: 33
EPS growth rate: 50%
FAIR maximum P/E at this growth rate: 50

"See, Caroline, when the earnings of a company are growing, stockholders are happy. It means the company is making money quickly and getting bigger. And that almost always means that the market price of a stock will go up. THAT's why people buy stock. They think its price will go up."

"Hey, even I can see that."

"And people who buy small, new, fast growing companies think that their price will go up faster than larger, older companies.'"

"Okay." I was with her so far.

"And if the earnings are growing at 50% a year, they're willing to pay a multiple of 50 for the stock! Understand?" She had apparently finished her explanation.

"I'm not sure. Are you saying that the 'multiple,' which is the stock's price divided by its earnings per share, is a number that should be the same as the company's growth rate?"

"Yes! Yes!," she cried. "You got it! And a P/E that's LOWER than the growth rate is even better." She paused.

"Well, I should say that the Caboodle clan always did well by paying stock prices that reflected companies' growth rates. It's when they paid multiples that were much HIGHER than the growth rate in earnings that they got hurt. So, if this little formula worked for the Caboodles, I think it's good enough for us, too."

KITT & CABOODLE'S COMMANDMENTS

5. Buy growth companies when the P/E is equal to or lower than the projected growth rate in earnings per share.

She paused. "I guess what bothers me is that raising the initial public offering price of Mom's Mums to $12 or even to $14 makes the stock's multiple much too high for its growth rate."

"Growth rate of 50%, right? Multiple of 50 would be about the right one?" I wanted to make sure I understood this.

"Yeah. And $12 is a multiple of 60. Fourteen dollars is a multiple of 70. Good grief. Much too expensive."

"Well, then, people just won't buy it, I guess, if it costs too much," I said.

"Maybe not. But a lot of people ignore the Caboodles' rule and pay multiples that are just crazy. Then, if the earnings don't come in as estimated or there's some little glitch in a company's business, the stock is just dumped by those guys. Price plummets." Kitt shuddered.

"I'd sure hate to have any of *my* clients holding stock in Mom's, having paid too much money for it to begin with, see the price drop way down. I HATE to lose other people's money. It's probably the thing I hate most in the world."

That's when I knew for certain that Kitt was an A #1 stockbroker. She cared deeply about such things as losing her customers' money *and* thought little about how much she herself made on the commissions. After all, commissions are paid when stock is bought and when stock is sold, so Kitt would make money whether the customer did or not.

Well, as it turned out, Kitt didn't have to worry about the price of Mom's getting out of line. After an all-nighter meeting between Mom, the investment bankers of Caboodle & Company, and the other lead managers, they decided to offer the stock to the public at the originally discussed $10 a share.

"The company is expected to earn 30 cents this year, remember? Take the 20 cents it earned last year and the 45 cents the analysts say it's likely to earn next year and we have an average growth rate of 50%"

"If the earnings estimates are correct," I interjected.

"You're learning. Baby companies are notoriously hard to predict. But Mona has a good shot at it."

"Okay," I began. "The multiple" — Kitt gave me an encouraging look — "is 50 based on last year's earnings. 'Multiple equal to or lower than the growth rate,'" I quoted our rule. "And since the growth rate is 50%, that's a fair price?"

"Yes. But most people will use this year's and next year's estimates. That may be pretty optimistic, but that's what they do."

"So on this year's estimate, Mom's is selling at a multiple of 33 and, on next year's, a paltry 22. Wow! Whadda buy!" I said. "Let's get some for our first investment."

"Caroline!" She looked at me as if I'd suggested running naked through the Caboodle & Company trading room. "You know we can't do that. We're 'insiders.'"

"Oh, phooey." She was right. When a stock is hot — and heaven knows this one was — people who are involved in any way with the investment bankers cannot legally buy it through the offering. After the 1929 Crash, a bunch of securities laws were passed to regulate the securities business so that people couldn't manipulate the stock market as easily anymore.

Keeping insiders out of the initial offering is one way of assuring that the initial offering price will be fair. Later, when a stock is trading publicly, it's perfectly legal for these "insiders" to buy it.

As for Mom's Mums, customers were clamoring for shares; there just weren't enough to satisfy the demand.

"How about if we buy some on the open market?" Kitt said. "As soon as the stock starts trading, I'll put in our order. Whaddya say to 200 shares?"

"That's $2000, right?"

"Plus the commission. It's figured into the price when people buy the initial public offering, but it's separate from the price when the stock is traded afterward.

"And keep in mind, it probably won't stay at 10."

"Right. Remember Netscape? Offered at 23 and shot up to 75 the first day it was traded. And it didn't have ANY earnings. No matter how excited we are about Mona's company, I don't want us to pay a higher multiple than the growth rate. Okay? Caboodle did that a couple of times and was sorry later. He says right in these papers" — she grabbed a few and waved them in the air — "'to wait until the price stabilizes.'"

Well, the Mom's Mums deal went well. It really put Caboodle & Company back on the map. We went from one broker to a whole team of brokers. The research department was resurrected from the dead and suddenly had a reputation for understanding "specialty retailing companies." Mr. C was now out with his cousin, beating the bushes for more corporate finance work. We were on the road again.

And after a week or two, when the price of Mom's Mums got back down to 12 (it had indeed shot up to 18 that first day of trading), we bought the stock. Based on the 30 cent earnings estimate, we paid a price-earnings ratio of 40, which is lower than the company's growth rate. And, based on next year's earnings estimate of 45 cents, we paid a "multiple" (or "P/E") of a mere 26.

Kitt and I carefully entered the following information on Mom's Mums in our joint-account notebook, along with the date of purchase:

200 MUMS @ 12

Reasons to own:

1. Excellent Management
2. Expanding markets carefully
3. Adding catalog business by first quarter this year
4. Building distribution center to increase market

The morning after we bought the stock, Kitt said to me, "Of course, the problem with the fair-price formula — you know, 'P/E should be equal to or less than the growth rate' — is that the growth rate is always based on someone's *estimate.* So we have to watch carefully."

"Naturally," I cut in. "It's a baby," and continued to sort Mr. C's mail.

So I began to watch carefully. I couldn't resist checking Kitt's Quotron machine (this is the box of technology that sat on every broker's

desk and hooked each up with up-to-the-second financial information all day long) every time I walked by her desk to see what the price of Mom's Mums was. I would type in the symbol ("MUMS") and the quoted bid (what the traders would pay me for the stock if we were to sell it) and asking prices (what we would have to pay the traders if we were buying more) would come up on the screen. The difference between these two prices is the "spread," which is just another name for commission, so far as I can see.

Mom's Mums was selling "over the counter" as part of NASDAQ (National Association of Securities Dealers' Automated Quote system) instead of being listed on one of the exchanges, like the New York or the American Stock Exchange. Caboodle & Company was "making a market" in the stock, meaning that we held it in inventory, just like a store that sells a certain brand of shoes.

The stock exchanges (the NYSE and the ASE are the largest and most important, but there are smaller regional exchanges, too) are auction markets. That is, buyers and sellers bid for shares of a company and do their transactions with the help of "floor" brokers, who are standing around on the actual floors of the exchanges, matching buyers' orders to sellers' orders. (I always thought it was funny that Caboodle owned a "seat" on the Exchange, since nobody sits and there aren't any chairs.) All this activity is computerized now and enormous amounts of stock change hands quickly because of that technology.

In order to be listed and traded on the New York Stock Exchange, there are a lot of stringent requirements for a company. It has to have a certain high level of sales, for example, and a certain number of shareholders. (When a stock is publicly traded, the Securities and Exchange Commission, or SEC, and the National Association of Securities Dealers, NASD, have their own long list of requirements for both the stock and the people who trade it.)

If a company fails to meet the standards of the NYSE while it's listed there, it will be "de-listed" or removed. Drummed out of the Corps, so to speak.

When a stock is "listed," that is, selling on a stock exchange, the commission is added to the price separately.

People sometimes get confused about this commission/spread stuff.

They think that there's no commission on an over-the-counter stock because it isn't shown separately on their confirmation slips (those little invoices that customers get in the mail, confirming that stock was bought or sold).

That just means that the firm they bought it from makes a market in the stock and no *additional* commission is charged. If you buy an over-the-counter stock from a firm that doesn't make a market in a stock, you pay the spread *and* a commission, too.

The "over-the-counter" market is not in one location, the way the exchanges are. Lots of dealers across the country make up this market and many now are part of the National Association of Securities Dealers Automated Quotation System (NASDAQ). With the help of computer technology, bid and asked prices on OTC stocks are flashed across the System by those people who are "making a market" or keeping an inventory and doing business in the stocks.

For instance, the Caboodle trader might offer to buy Mom's Mums stock at 15. This is called the "bid" price. At the same time, this trader could be offering to sell Mom's at 15 1/4. This is the "asked" price. (*Remember, the difference between the two prices is called "the spread."*) Anyway, this information is flashed all over the country on this NASDAQ system, so that anyone who's interested in the stock can immediately see which market-makers are offering it at what prices.

As it happened, several other major brokerage firms — besides us — were keeping an inventory or "making a market" in Mom's Mums. This was good because it meant that the stock would be talked about and, therefore, bought by more people.

With our purchase of Mom's, I was glad to get started on our investment portfolio. We had our baby company and I was certainly a conscientious babysitter, what with punching in the symbol every fifteen minutes and sweating out price swings from 12 to 11 to 9, and then up to 12 again, the same day.

"Uh, Caroline," Kitt began, as I leaned over her and began to enter MUMS. I think you may have misunderstood when I said, 'Watch the company like you'd watch a baby.' I didn't mean to watch the *stock price.* I meant that we should watch what the company is doing and how its business is going and all that. The stock can act crazy some days."

"Why does it do that?"

"These daily fluctuations happen with a small company. There are so few shares out there that institutional buying and selling is going to make the price go up and down a lot. If we like the company and the way business is being done there, and if our reasons for buying Mom's haven't changed, I say we stop looking at the price." She fixed me with a stern look. "Okay?"

I thought about this for a minute. "Shouldn't we sell the stock if it goes up to, say, fifteen or twenty?" I knew the answer, but couldn't help asking the question.

Kitt looked really exasperated. "Good Lord, Caroline, NO. Remember Caboodle's Commandment #3? 'You only sell when the reasons you bought the company are no longer valid.' We're *supposed* to be long term investors.

"Here's another thing that Caboodle said" — Kitt was now returning to the pile of papers on her desk and drawing one out — 'Short term moves in the capital markets are random; long term moves are rational.' He actually wrote that a lot, so he must have felt the need to remind *himself* of it, too."

"Well," I said, backing away from the Quotron, "we want to be rational, too, so I guess we hold for the long term. Okay. I'll stop checking the price." I walked over to my desk and leaned against it. "But it sure is tempting."

CHAPTER FOUR: SETTLING IN

What To Buy Next?

I sat down, pushed a few papers around on my desk and then popped The Logical Big Question, "So what do we buy next?"

We'd invested about $2400, including the spread, and had a long way to go before we could call our little stash a "portfolio."

"I've been thinking about that," said Kitt, who was studying a page of Caboodle-lore, her brow furrowed. "This is good stuff. Right here, the old guy put down a formula we can still use."

"Yeah?" I like formulas. Especially from the ultra-rich on how to get that way. "What is it?"

"He wrote, 'First know what the *purpose* is for the portfolio. Second, know its *time horizon.* Third, know how much *money is available to invest.* Fourth, know how much *risk* is acceptable. And, fifth, know what the *tax considerations* are,'" Kitt read.

"Wow. That's great. Just about covers it, don't you think?" I said in amazement.

"It sure does. Okay," Kitt said, "What is our purpose?"

"To build up a retirement fund. I mean, that's mine. Isn't it yours?"

"Yup. And our time horizon?"

"Well, I guess if we split the difference in our ages, about 25 to 30 years."

"In other words, a long time horizon. Right?" Kitt asked.

"Long." I agreed.

"And the money we have available is coming in as we work for it. But we still have some of our original pot left — about $20,000, right?"

"A little more."

"How much risk is acceptable?" Kitt asked, then answered her own

question. "We can take reasonable risks because we have time to make up losses."

"Yup. And our portfolio is fully-taxed."

"But remember that capital gains build up tax-deferred in stocks."

"What do you mean?"

"It's another good reason for holding common stocks. Until we sell it, we don't have to pay tax on stock that goes up," Kitt said. I knew that.

"Now that we know all these things, does old Caboodle tell us what we do next?"

"No, but I can figure it out. We want to buy more common stocks. We want to take reasonable risks. We want to be *patient*," Kitt said in a firm voice. "We need to put the rest of our portfolio to work — so I'd better do some more homework."

Kitt went back to her reading. I returned to my work. After a few minutes, she got up and went over to the big green notebooks we have on a shelf just inside the front door. She looked something up. Then she pulled out the navy blue books and thumbed through them purposefully. She wrote something down on a piece of paper and returned to her desk.

"Okay," she said, looking down at the notes she had made. "I think we should balance the risk of owning this baby company of Mom's by purchasing shares in an adult company, okay? I like the predictability of a blue chip company like Kicky Kola. It's expanding globally, too. Most of its earnings come from its overseas business."

Remembering the Caboodle Rule, I said, "Okay, there are a couple of reasons for buying this stock: predictability of earnings and international expansion. What are some others?"

"Uh … solid balance sheet, manageable debt load, A+ rating by Standard & Poor's."

"Excuse me?"

"Caboodle never bought a company with more than 40% debt out of its total capital. See, you don't want the interest payments the company has to make on its outstanding debt — like bonds — to be too high. If revenue goes down because of a recession or something, it might be too hard to cover those loan payments and earn something, too. Companies have even gone bankrupt because they couldn't pay their

debts. But Kicky Kola has less than 20% debt out of its total capital," she said.

"For heaven's sake, how did you find *that* out?" I asked.

"It's right there in *Value Line*," she gestured to the big blue *Value Line* book. I regularly stuff updates of investment information into those things but, of course, had never read it. Kitt reached over to a pile of papers and took the top one: Kicky Kola's *Value Line* report. "See?" she asked, pointing to the left margin. "Right here in the parentheses, it says, 20%."

"How did they come up with that?" I asked, puzzled by all this math.

"Wait a minute, I'll tell you. You take the long term debt, add it to the value of the common stock, and you get the total capital for the company. You have to have that total amount in order to figure out what percentage of it is represented by the long-term debt. Got that?" Kitt asked.

"Yeah. That's not so hard. I do that with my paycheck a lot. You know, figure out what percentage has to go to pay my regular bills."

"Right."

"So it looks like the long-term debt for Kicky Kola is ..." I tapped out the numbers on my little calculator, "... 20%. Just like it says."

"See how easy it is?" Kitt asked. I nodded.

"Just to make sure a company can pay its bills, it's a good idea to do another little test, too. It's called the 'quick ratio,' I guess because you can do it quickly."

"Okay, what's that?" I asked, feeling smugly mathematical and ready for anything now that I could figure out debt to total capital.

"That one's really simple. You just take the current assets listed on the balance sheet — those would be the cash and marketable securities — and match them to the current liabilities, listed under the same name."

"This makes so much *sense*," I said.

"It should be at least a one-to-one match. You know, even up. Two-to-one is even better."

"They should have the cash to pay for their current bills, is what you're saying."

"You got it. If the cash number is higher than the liabilities number, naturally that's no problem. But if it's lower, get worried."

She went on, "No problem with good old Kicky Kola, of course. But I also looked at the S&P tearsheets to find out how it ranks Kicky." She pointed to the other notebooks. "A+, as advertised."

Good old *Value Line* and S&P. Kitt told me that they're the investor's best friends when it comes to good research. They do your homework for you. At Caboodle & Company, we give these things to customers. "*Value Line* reports" and "S&P tearsheets" they're called. All a customer has to do is ask her broker for them, but both are also available at most public libraries. They're the next best thing to having your own research department. In fact, Kitt always checks *Value Line* and S&P against what the analysts in our research department are saying, to confirm or refute their opinions on a stock.

Of course, Mom's Mums was too new to be in either *Value Line* or *Standard & Poor's.* A company's stock needs to have attracted a lot of interest before it'll be followed by either publication. (Interest is measured by the number of shares that trade each day.)

"Another reason why baby companies are risky," Kitt said when I brought this up. "You're relying on only one or two sources of information about the companies' prospects."

Caboodle & Company Expands and Kitt Learns About Research

Kitt was tireless, as usual. She was sort of the unofficial sales manager and recruiter of new stockbrokers. In my opinion, by the time she'd been with us for a couple of years, Kitt knew more about the business than some guys who'd been lashed to Quotron machines for half their lives. Her advantage was the Caboodle papers, and her unstoppable interest in finding out, partly through them, exactly how things worked in the investment business. I mean, she *had* to know EVERYTHING.

Take the BASIL business. "Basil" is the name of a restaurant chain that had gone public about eight years before. Caboodle did the offering, one of the last big ones before the brokers walked and our business nearly disintegrated. It was "BK: Before Kitt."

After Kitt bought us both Mom's Mums and Kicky Kola stock, we

were casting around for another growth company to own. We both liked the idea of buying shares in a teenage company, so I suggested we consider Basil as the next stock to buy for our portfolio.

Basil's owner, also named Basil, chose Caboodle to do the IPO partly because our research analyst, Harry Hill, knew a lot about restaurants. Harry had known Basil for years and understood what it took to make money in the restaurant business. He thought Basil was a real comer.

Basil owned and operated a restaurant in our city, so, the day after the company went public, Mr. C took Harry, six of the retail brokers, and me to Basil's for lunch. The place was jammed. The food was great. We toasted Basil, Caboodle & Company, each other, the food, the menu, the fine service, and were down to honoring the clean restrooms when Mr. C finally paid the bill and we left. It was a grand afternoon.

By the time Kitt came to the firm, Basil had become a well-known chain of medium-priced restaurants, popular with yuppie-type families who were reproducing rapidly. Its local restaurant was still always jammed with parents, young children, and retired types who liked the food, the prices, and the good service.

On the basis of Harry's research and our local Basil's, we bought 200 shares and popped it into the portfolio, along with our reasons to own: excellent management, consistent earnings growth, popularity with baby boomers, reasonably priced, good quality food, and expansion potential in other cities.

But something was happening to Basil in other cities. One morning, after returning from a trip to see her cousins in North Carolina, Kitt said to me, "I was so disappointed, Caroline. I took the whole bunch to Basil's and it was awful: the service was slow and the bathroom was dirty. The food wasn't even good."

"You should tell Harry about that, Kitt," I said, nervously. "The stock is on our recommended list. He ought to know if the other restaurants in the chain aren't as good as ours."

So Kitt told Harry, whose star had risen because of the IPO's success. He seemed only mildly disturbed. In fact, as Kitt later replayed the conversation to me, he was more disturbed with *her* than with the lousy restaurant.

"That North Carolina unit, he said, wasn't owned by the company. It was owned by a franchisee, like a lot of the units. I asked, 'Didn't Basil have any way to control the quality of the restaurants he didn't own?' He just looked at me like I was a cowpie in a punchbowl." I winced at the description.

"Oh, sorry," Kitt said. She went on in a puzzled tone, "But he was really sort of mad at me."

"He's got a lot at stake with Basil. The company comes to Caboodle whenever it needs to offer more stock. It's a very big client and Harry's bonus depends a lot on his ability to bring in this bit of corporate finance business," I told her.

"But he still should know if there's a problem, shouldn't he? I mean, he's telling people to buy the stock ..." Kitt stopped. "Uh-oh. Wait a minute. You mean, because the guy is a corporate finance client, *WE* aren't getting the right story here?" Her voice was rising.

"Ssshhhh. Listen, this sort of thing isn't unusual at all. Everybody knows about it. The research analyst who brings in banking business is the company star, and gets paid on the basis of that business. It's hard for him to turn around and say that things aren't as good as they used to be. Happens everywhere on Wall Street."

"Well, so what are we supposed to do? I mean, who do we believe? We own this thing, remember?" Her voice was again rising.

I remembered only too well. It was one-third of our holdings. I felt the rising tide of panic, but fought it back, saying, "Well, first of all, one visit to one franchise doesn't mean that Basil is going to the dogs. This unit could be new ..."

"It isn't."

"Okay, so maybe it was just a bad day. I wouldn't come to any big conclusions until you've done some more homework," I cautioned.

Kitt walked away, muttering to herself about conflicts of interest. She was discovering something that all brokers discover eventually and that I should have remembered in our frenzy to buy another company for our portfolio: you can't believe everything you hear about a stock, especially if what you hear is always good and especially if the company uses *yours* when it wants to offer more stock to the public. Good brokers must learn which analysts have the guts to tell the truth. Of course, those are often

the ones on the "remember" list, as in "Remember John Jones? He *USED* to be our such and such analyst."

Stockbrokers and The Royal Georges

Thanks to Kitt, our sales force of retail stockbrokers had grown substantially. We now had twelve guys and one woman, Kitt — about the same ratio of men to women as in the industry itself. Why women represent less than 10 percent of the total, I'm not sure. Stockbrokering is a great business for a woman. (The only reason I don't do it is because I started out as this one-woman back office and liked it. A lot. I don't want to change and start all over. And I'm too scared to live on commission only, which is what you have to do as a broker.)

Anyway, a couple of these hotshot new brokers decided they didn't want to deal with what they considered to be "small clients" anymore. You know, people like you and me, the "individual investor" who's the retail stockbroker's customer.

So they asked Mr. C and he said "yes" to their request to do business only with institutions. "Institutional investors" are any accounts over, say, $50 million. For some reason, these accounts are considered "firm accounts," meaning they belong to Caboodle & Company, while accounts like Kitt's and mine are the broker's own, part of his or her "book," and can't be taken away by any other broker.

Mr. C is the only one who can assign the big institutional accounts to a broker. Those big guy investors are supposed to be so smart they need some specially-trained, more *sophisticated* dude to talk to them. And it's those huge institutional accounts that do most of the trading on any given day. They're responsible for pretty nearly all the activity on Wall Street.

So these stockbrokers had asked Mr. C if they could be the ones to call on the people who manage huge amounts of money, generally for other people, like pension plans, insurance companies, mutual funds, wealthy families, endowment funds. He said yes and boy, did they get snooty.

There's a sort of hierarchy in the sales force here. Probably it exists in every brokerage firm. There aren't any real promotions, like climbing the corporate ladder to the presidency. A broker is judged by the size of his or her customers and the resulting commissions. So an institutional broker feels like he/she is a few rungs up the ladder from the retail guy who's dealing with ordinary folks, doing a hundred shares at a time or putting $1000 into a mutual fund. That's because the institutional guy is buying a hundred THOUSAND shares at a time or spending A MILLION DOLLARS, and his customer is a mutual fund.

Of course, some retail brokers work with customers who have many millions to invest, too. Usually, it's because the broker began investing for these people back when they were young and just starting out. So they sort of grew together. It's hard for a new young broker to get that kind of big customer normally.

Anyway, our two institutional brokers are both named George: George Jenkins and George Cutter. Mr. C calls them "the Georges." Kitt calls them "the Royals." So now I think of them as "the Royal Georges." Kitt told me that, in the sales meetings, they delight in grilling the analysts with questions like, "What's the turnover ratio in sales? And, why are same-store sales weak?" Of course, the analysts usually know the answers, but aren't used to telling them to retail brokers. They think that regular-people customers don't care about such things.

After one of these sessions, Kitt came out of the room, looking fierce. She stood by her desk, watching people disperse and then, when the Royal Georges appeared, walked up to them resolutely.

"Can I talk to you guys?" she asked.

George Jenkins looked at her, then at his watch. "For a minute," he said. George Cutter said nothing, just walked over to his desk in silence, as if she hadn't spoken. Kitt stifled whatever laser-like retort she had in mind and asked, "Sit a minute?" gesturing to the seat by her desk.

"Okay. What can I do for you?" George sat.

"Listen, George. I'm worried about the Basil stock. We don't get anything but nice little stories from these analysts and now you say" — Kitt consulted her notes — "that the 'same store sales are down.' How did you find that out?" Kitt asked earnestly.

George looked uncomfortable. "Well, if you want to know the truth, my customer told me."

"What?"

"Yeah. I was pretty embarrassed that she knew more about it than I did. I can tell you, Kitt," said George, wiggling a little in his chair, "these institutional investors are really on top of things. We've got to get better information or George and I will get eaten alive."

Kitt looked over at the other George's desk. "What a good idea," she murmured.

"Huh?" George said.

"Uh ... it would be a good idea for all of us to know more, I think," Kitt said.

"Oh, you guys don't need to know that stuff. Your customers don't care," George sniffed.

"Look, George. Just because our customers are smaller than yours doesn't mean their *brains* are. Stop acting like we're numbskulls. If same-store sales figures are going to hurt the stock, ALL the customers need to understand that."

George looked abashed. "I didn't mean to sound ..."

"Yeah, you did. You do. And so does the other George. You're getting to be pains in the rear, if you want to know the truth. But that's not the problem here. *This* is the problem: what are 'same store sales figures' and why are they important?"

George looked at her for a brief moment and then laughed. Kitt laughed, too. "I'd really appreciate your telling me about this stuff, George. It bothers the heck out of me that there's so much I don't know and that my customers think I do."

"Same store sales," he began, "are what the restaurants that have been up and running for a while are doing *now* in sales, compared to what they were doing this quarter last year."

"What *should* they be?" Kitt asked as she continued writing in her notebook.

"Well, same store sales should be up, not down. Sales figures for the whole Basil chain are up, but as my customer pointed out to me" — George looked pained — "that's because Basil keeps adding new stores and the new units do pretty well at first."

"So the real test as to whether Basil's earnings are growing is the same-store number?"

"Yeah. And it isn't good," George said glumly. "I gotta go." He got up and walked back to his desk.

"Thanks," Kitt said to his retreating figure. She stared after him for a few minutes, deep in thought. Then she pushed her chair back, stood up and, taking her notebook under her arm, marched into Mr. C's office.

A few minutes later, Kitt returned, looking anxious and smug at the same time. "I'm moving my desk next to the Royals," she whispered. "I can learn a lot by listening to them talk on the phone. When it comes to training, Caboodle & Company sure is a do-it-yourself operation," she muttered as she sat at her desk, pulling open drawers and lifting out their contents.

So Kitt moved next to the Royal Georges and began to ask questions at the morning research meetings that sounded just like theirs: she wanted to know all kinds of things about the companies that the research analysts followed and recommended as good investments.

"Basically, Caroline, I just want to find out what can go WRONG," she explained to me one day over coffee in our employees' lounge.

"So, what went wrong with Basil?"

"I think they tried to expand too fast — opened too many new units without paying attention to the old ones. Forgot about quality control, too. Since Harry is so reluctant to say anything bad about the company, I'm doing a little research on my own."

"How are you doing *that?*" I asked, pouring myself another cup of coffee.

"I'm activating my network of informants — the Kitt family. We're all over the place." Kitt's face broke into that smile. "I've got cousins in the East, the South, in California and Texas and, of course, in Nebraska. There are Kitts in Maine and in Florida too." She pushed her chair back, walked over and closed the door. Then she sat down again and said, "I sent them all a letter asking for them to go eat in their local Basil and enclosed a list of things for them to ask the manager."

"Well, how about that! When did you do that?"

"Last week. I should be hearing back anytime now. Some of them have faxes, some are on-line, most will probably call me. I told them I needed the information quickly."

It's amazing what a little field research can do. Within the week, the

Kitt family spy ring was reporting in via fax, E-mail, the U.S. Postal Service, and the phone. Their reviews of Basil were decidedly mixed, too.

"Cousin Cam from San Francisco tells me that the manager was nowhere to be found, he wasn't served for an hour, and there were mistakes on his check. Tom Kitt from Colorado had a good time at his Basil, but he works so hard he hasn't been to a restaurant for five years, and probably doesn't have real high standards. But he said the food was good, the manager was cordial, and that it was owned by the company, not a franchisee. Oh, and his wife thanks me for the night out."

Kitt smiled and looked up from the fax she was reading. "That seems to be the key, that franchisee thing. When a Basil is owned by Basil, the quality is usually terrific."

In a few days, Kitt's network of underground researchers had caused her Basil file to practically overflow, and she decided to show the nationwide assessment to Harry Hill.

"He's not going to be happy with me," she said, "but I think he ought to know what's going on."

"So what do *you* think is going on?" I again asked.

"Just what I thought to begin with. I'm pretty sure that Basil expanded too fast, took on too many franchisees without checking them out carefully. He was too eager to see his restaurants spread from coast-to-coast, even if they weren't company-owned. See, these people can buy the name and get a lot of start-up help from the company when they become franchisees, but they're actually independent operators, bearing the Basil name but outside of Basil's complete control as far as their quality is concerned.

So Kitt took her information to Harry Hill and, as predicted, he wasn't happy. He called Basil, and talked to some of his pals at the restaurant chain. Sure enough, they acknowledged that there was "weakness in the franchisee-owned units," meaning that a lot of them were turkeys, but they insisted that things are "on track," whatever that means. I'd sure be happier if the management had some plan for taking care of this "weakness."

"So what's Harry going to do about it?" I asked.

"Ha! Listen to this: he told us today that he was 'lowering his recommendation for Basil from a strong buy to a hold.'"

"A hold?

"Yeah. That's analyst-speak for 'sell this dog, it's going nowhere but I can't say that in English,'" Kitt said. "Lucky most of us speak 'analyst' and know what he means. Pity the poor broker who actually thinks Harry *MEANS* to 'hold.'"

Kitt earned Harry's respect that day. But any chances of her becoming his new best friend went out the window. In some parts of Caboodle & Company, Kitt and her network of cousins became known as the KGB, and she personally as Comrade Kittsky. The other research analysts watched her warily and started to provide more detailed reports during morning meetings in order to keep her from activating her network of sleuths.

Mr. C, as usual, knew nothing about all of this and was heard to ask, "Kittsky? Why do you call her Kittsky, Harry?" as the two walked within earshot of Kitt's desk one day.

Actually, Kitt hadn't been all that popular to start with. The analysts hadn't paid her any attention at all, just nodded vaguely to her when passing each other in the halls of Caboodle & Company. Some even assumed she was a secretary (or "sales support," as those dauntless women are called in this age of enlightenment). Now they knew.

So the question I had for Kitt was, "What should we do with our Basil stock?" It was a teenager company: "Wasn't this franchise thing just part of its growing pains?"

"I don't think so, Caroline. I think it was an important failure of management. 'Quality Control' is a big part of its job.

"Remember our reasons to own Basil? 'Excellent management, consistent earnings growth, popularity with baby boomers, reasonably priced, good quality food, and expansion potential.' Well, none of those things will be true if the franchises are awful and the food and service at their restaurants are lousy." She sighed.

"It's a tough call. If the management is as good as we thought they were, they'll eventually clear up these problems. But it's hard to do that quickly enough in as competitive a business as restaurants. I'd rather sell Basil now before we lose more money.

"We can buy it again if we see good hard evidence that the management understands its problems and is willing to do something

about them."

So we sold our Basil stock. Originally, we had bought 200 shares at 15 and sold it at 10. Ouch! We lost about a thousand dollars on it, but would have lost more had we held on.

The other retail brokers at Caboodle & Company loved the whole Basil caper and started to put in requests for kick-the-tires, on-the-scene research of other questionable companies. I learned an important lesson from the experience: It's altogether possible for regular people like me, Kitt, and Kitt's cousins to do so-called "primary research" on companies merely by using plain old common sense.

KITT & CABOODLE'S COMMANDMENTS

6. Know what can go wrong
before investing in a company.

CHAPTER FIVE: FIGURING IT OUT

KITT COMES UP WITH HER PLAN

Kitt was developing her business nicely, appearing before all kinds of groups, with audiences of young, old, and in-between. Inevitably, after she gave one of her talks, people came up and asked for her advice on how they should invest.

"You know, it just isn't as easy as saying, 'Buy this' or 'Buy that,'" she told me once. "You need to know a lot about people before you can give them good advice.

"How, for example, would they feel if a stock went down after they bought it, like us with Basil? And how long are they going to keep their stock before selling it? And do they need income to live on? Lots of things like that." She looked at me. "How would *you* answer those questions?"

"I feel very nervous when our stock goes down. But I feel just as nervous when I see it go up, believe it or not," I answered with a laugh.

"Good reason for not looking at it all the time, right?" Kitt replied. "We want to hold these things for a long time. At least I do. Don't you?"

"Yeah. Years and years. So how often *should* we look at our stocks?"

"Looking carefully at the monthly statements (to make sure everything is accurate), and reading the quarterly reports should be often enough. We both read the business pages." Kitt looked at me. "You DO read the business pages of the newspaper, *don't you*?"

"I do now. Never used to. But I'm finding it interesting now. I got a subscription to *Business Week*, too."

"Good. You read *Business Week* and *Forbes*. I'll read the *Wall Street Journal* and *Investors' Business Daily*. And we'll both read the daily paper. We'll be reasonably well-informed about the business climate then."

"*I'm* going to add a rule, okay?" I asked Kitt. She looked pleased.

"Sure … what is it?"

"Read more. About business."

"Good one. It's useful to get a lot of different perspectives on what's happening in the business world."

KITT & CABOODLE'S COMMANDMENTS

7. Read for ten to thirty extra minutes a day: Wall Street Journal, New York Times Business section, Investors' Business Daily, Business Week, Forbes, Barron's, Fortune, etc.

ENTER THE McWEEDIES

About this time, a couple called the McWeedies showed up in Kitt's life. They were retirees who'd attended one of her seminars on "How to Invest" and later came in to talk to her about their investment portfolio.

Mr. McWeedie had worked for the phone company all his life — well, all his grownup life, anyway. He was short and round with a wide, handlebar moustache and walked with a limp. Mrs. McWeedie had been a librarian before she retired. She, too, was also a little rickety on her feet, and lurched from side to side when walking, even though Mr. McWeedie held her firmly under the elbow as they moved around in tandem.

Neither McWeedie was more than five feet tall. They looked like a pair of bookends, standing in front of my desk one morning, asking for "Missy Kitt, please?"

I pointed out Kitt's desk. She was huddled over a pile of the old papers, puzzling over some distant Caboodle coup. She looked up and smiled broadly. The McWeedies limped and lurched across the floor, calling, "Hello there! Do you have time for us?"

"Absolutely! But let's go into a conference room. There's no room

out here." She looked over at me and I nodded toward one of the private rooms used for these customer meetings.

"The Dining Room is available," I said. That room was called the Dining Room because the wall was hung from floor to ceiling with framed tombstone notices of IPOs done by Caboodle & Company during its glory days. Most of the companies were restaurant chains, fast food companies, places to eat.

The two little McWeedies and Kitt disappeared into the Dining Room. Later, Kitt told me they'd asked her to help them invest the lump sums they each received at retirement. Seems all this cash was sitting in a certificate of deposit somewhere, barely earning enough money to feed a parking meter, much less a couple of adult human beings.

"The rate of inflation is higher than the interest they're earning," Kitt said. "They're actually losing money in purchasing power."

"So what did you tell them to do?" I asked.

"That I'd have to think about it a little more. The McWeedies need monthly income, but they also need to have some money in common stocks so that this retirement lump sum won't shrink up to nothing. CDs just won't do it for them."

So Kitt immersed herself in the Caboodle papers again to see how the Greats had tackled this problem.

"What was their secret?" she asked me over and over. It was a rhetorical question, of course, since the Caboodles had never seen fit to confide their innermost thoughts to their wire operator.

"Maybe they just got lucky. You know, the Dartboard Theory?" People always joke about the fact that an investor can do better throwing darts at a list of stocks and buying the ones they hit, than taking the advice of investment professionals.

"Nah. They knew something. There's a pattern. There's a key. I'll figure it out ... but it's really bugging me."

What an interesting idea, I thought. A "Key to the Caboodle Oodles" locked away in the Caboodle papers for all these years, while the current generation's Mr. C wandered around his office, presiding over a shrinking business. I guess this investment know-how didn't come with the name, or maybe the Caboodle line had thinned in the steamy air of orchid-growing. It was just a pity that poor Mr. C hadn't organized and

read those papers himself years ago.

Kitt came in very early those mornings and stayed late. The McWeedies were waiting and she knew how much they needed good advice. She looked tired, her smile hanging onto her face briefly before sliding off and leaving a puzzled frown.

"They trust me to do the right thing," Kitt murmured one morning when I suggested that she needed a good night's sleep. "HOW did the C's set things up so they could all go off to various islands and retire," forever as it turned out.

"Well, in the old days, I don't think any of them lived much more than a couple of years beyond retirement. And keeping up with inflation wasn't a big issue for early Caboodles, either."

As she continued to read, I thought, "Those McWeedies, for all their limping and lurching, had looked pretty healthy and very likely to be around for years to come. Maybe Kitt should tell them to go back to work. Sixty-five is too early to retire anyway."

"I agree," said Kitt after I passed along this latest brainstorm. "But there must be another solution." She gestured to the files and papers that littered her desk.

"That's why I keep after these Caboodle papers. Those guys knew how to make money. Their fortune kept growing through good times and bad. I've learned at least one thing. Everybody should own at least some common stocks with earnings growth, no matter how old they are."

"That sounds like another rule to me," I said.

"It sure is."

KITT & CABOODLE'S COMMANDMENTS

8. Always own some *common stocks whose earnings are growing. That's the best way to maintain your purchasing power and to defend against inflation.*

She returned to her reading, saying, "I told the McWeedies, 'CDs and money market funds aren't investments. It's like putting your car in a garage. You can park it or you can drive it somewhere. And the only way to get someplace is to take it out of the garage.'"

I confessed to Kitt that, before I had met her, there were so many stocks and investment options to choose from that I ended up not choosing anything for my teeny-weeny investment portfolio, which — as she had said it would — had stayed about the same since I had bought treasury bonds with it several years earlier. (This, of course, was outside of the money that I gave the Caboodle & Company broker who didn't know any more than I did.)

"So, instead of taking a chance on anything, now I just leave it in treasuries," I said. "Very much like the McWeedies."

"You've taken a chance without knowing it. That money is worth less today than when you first got it. Five thousand dollars just isn't the same as it used to be. You've *got* to buy common stocks," Kitt said firmly. "I rest my case."

"Easy for you to say. There are a million stocks to choose from. I never knew which ones to buy." I looked at her and smiled. "But I'm learning. We don't have to buy them *all*, do we? Just a few good choices."

Kitt smiled. "The point is to buy *something*. Get started. Don't just let the money sit there. Parked."

She returned to her reading. But instead of settling into the job, she opened and closed a few of the files, seemingly unable to concentrate. Finally, she looked up at me and said, "Caroline, my garden is just beginning to look pretty good and I need to show it off. Why don't you knock off and come visit? I need a break from this stuff."

Kitt's Garden

It was almost 5:30, so I closed up shop and followed her out the door. We walked along the downtown streets, cutting through office buildings and across a small park, against the tide of homebound office workers and late afternoon traffic, towards Kitt's little apartment, which was in an old home built on Murphy Square. She had the ground floor with a nice

patch of land fenced in behind it.

While Kitt poured iced tea into a couple of glasses, I complimented her on her garden. There was color everywhere, along with some well-trimmed shrubs and small trees. Kitt was thumbing through her mail, mostly colorful ads. "Did you plant all those flowers?" I asked.

"Yup. Mom helped me with good advice. She always has something blooming in her garden, Spring, Summer and Fall." We carried the icy glasses out to her tiny porch and settled into the two wooden chairs facing the yard.

"So I've tried to do the same thing. I had a lot of stuff coming up in the Spring. Now I'm working on the Summer part of the garden, planting lots of different kinds of bulbs and shrubs. It's nice because when one set of things is dormant, another will be blooming." She pointed to a couple of small trees at the back of the property.

"I've got the Fall stuff in place, too. This fall, I'll have apples from my fruit trees, if the squirrels don't get them first. I hope those chrysanthemums I put in will bloom. It's great to know that those things do well even if the weather is iffy."

Kitt put down her iced tea glass and looked up. "Caroline!" she yelled.

"What?"

"I've got it. The Caboodle Key. The Secret. I know what it is. In fact, I think I've known it all along. Investing is just like farming. It's just like I told my folks when I first started to work here … " She stood, her mail sliding to the floor.

"It's so simple that I can't believe it took me so long to figure it out. I even told my dad that the Caboodles had an all-weather way of looking at their investments, like farmers.

"It's like planting a garden, see?"

"No," I admitted.

"Well, in a garden, you plant things that will do well in each season, right?" She didn't wait for an answer. Warming to her subject, she began to pace.

"What hurts stock markets the most? Bad news, inflation, interest rates, economic stuff like that. What *helps* it the most? Same things — good news, low inflation and interest rates — economic stuff again.

"So, the way I see it, the seasons of the year are like economic climates. There are times when things are budding and growing fast — that's Spring.

"There are times when things bloom at different times, like they do in this garden. That's Summer.

"There are times when you don't know what the climate is going to be like, so you plant things that'll do well in chancy weather, like apples and mums. That's Fall.

"Then there are times when nothing blooms and everything is dormant. That's Winter. That's when you're happy to be inside where it's warm, looking out at the garden covered in snow. See?" She stopped pacing and looked at me intently.

"Yeah," I said, "but I'm not sure how that relates to the Caboodles. Or us."

"They *did* this. They probably wouldn't have said it that way, but that's what they were doing, planting a portfolio for all economic climates. Putting investments into place that they wouldn't have to trade around a lot and then, just sitting tight, knowing they were well-positioned, no matter what kind of season they were facing."

"So how do we do that? I mean, you and I in our joint portfolio?"

"First, we look at what we have and see where it fits."

"Okay. That's easy. We have Kicky Kola and Mom's Mums. An adult and a baby... ."

"GROWTH companies," Kitt finished. "They're budding and growing. So we've started our portfolio with Spring investments. We've got Summer covered, too. With an investment that has business all over the world, in places that don't all bloom at the same time."

"That would be Kicky Kola with all its international business?"

"Right. We might want to look into buying an international mutual fund to fully cover Summer. But owning Kicky is a good start."

"So what about the other seasons — Fall and Winter," I asked.

"Fall investments are like the Fall climate: transitional. They're good quality utilities, for example — good for both income and a little growth. And Winter investments would be things that contribute when nothing else is working out, like good quality bonds that pay interest even in hard times."

"Well, we should own some of those things too, right?" I asked.

"In due time," Kitt replied. "We'll buy things to cover those climates when we've done our homework on them. No matter what these other brokers do, I don't like to rush into anything I don't know much about. We've got time to do our homework. Remember that, Caroline."

She looked at me earnestly over her iced tea glass. "Don't let me rush you into anything, no matter how enthusiastic I get. We've got time to do our homework," she repeated.

The Four-Season Portfolio Plan

At the next sales meeting, Kitt introduced her portfolio planning technique. She explained it as "a way to defend your investments against changing economic climates." She called it, "The Four-Season Portfolio Plan."

"This plan is a way to set up a customer's portfolio so that it doesn't get destroyed by bad market conditions, so that you don't have to do a lot of trading when interest rates change, or a recession hits. Once you set it up, you're ready for just about anything."

At this point, the Royal Georges made their exit. A portfolio that you can't move around for commissions was of NO interest to them or their institutional customers. Quite a few other eyes glazed over, but she went on.

"Let's start with Spring. By Spring, I mean those times when the economy is starting to grow after a recession. The profits of companies are growing, too. So it's a good time to own growth stocks. That's the way to take advantage of Spring." She looked around to see if anyone disagreed.

"Next we have Summer. In a calendar year, it's the season when you have flowers popping up, one right after the other, all over the garden. But the irises don't bloom at the same time as the daisies or the day lilies. And neither do economies. I mean, European markets might be doing terribly, but South American stock markets could be booming. And if those two are doing badly, the Japanese market might be performing great. All these economies don't get strong *or* weak at once.

"So for Summer in your portfolio, you need to own some international investments. That way, you'll have something in bloom all the time."

She looked around and continued, "Next comes Fall."

"Fall?" asked one of the brokers, with a grin. "Is that when the whole thing falls apart?"

"Whoops. You're right. Never use the word 'Fall' when referring to your stock portfolio. Let's call this season Autumn," said Kitt.

"In the calendar year, Autumn is a season when you don't know what weather to expect. You know, it could get really warm one day and be really cold the next. It's a transition time, when you want to be prepared for anything. There are transitional times in the economy as well.

"I think that the best way to cover this transitional Autumn is with stocks that pay good dividends but still may grow a little — things like good quality utilities and well-managed real estate investment trusts.

"And with really good quality utilities and REITs, the dividends grow, too, at about the rate of inflation. That's a big help as people get into retirement. I'd put convertible bonds and convertible preferred stocks in Autumn too.

"The last season is Winter. During the actual season of Winter, nothing much is growing, and things are dormant, waiting for Spring. In our Four Season Portfolio Plan, there's an economic Winter. When companies' earnings aren't growing, it's hard to make money in stocks.

"For that kind of economic climate, it's good to own some bonds. The income from them is fixed. Interest will be paid twice a year, no matter what's happening outside: recession, depression, war, pestilence. And the money you put into the bonds comes back to you when they mature.

"Of course, the quality had better be high — like U.S. treasuries or triple-A corporate bonds. Naturally, people in a higher income tax bracket will prefer the triple-A, tax-free municipals to the taxable corporates or treasuries.

"But the quality needs to be excellent. You wouldn't want anything *flaky* for Winter, heh-heh-heh." Kitt looked around. Silence from the troops.

"So what do you think?" she asked.

"Sounds good. Sounds like it could work." Bill Baker rubbed his fore-

head — a sign that he was thinking. With Bill, you needed these outward signs.

"But it also sounds like the customer wouldn't need us once we set up their portfolio your way." Nothing, if not realistic, that Bill.

"I'm not so sure about that, Bill," said Walter Goodale. "If you do the right thing for your customers, they always seem to find more money for you to work with."

But the other brokers seemed to agree with Bill. They thanked Kitt for her idea, closed their notebooks and *Wall Street Journals* and filed out of the big basement room where the sales meetings were held. Kitt watched them go. I was there, taking notes for Mr. C, who always wanted to know what Kitt had to say. I saw the discouraged look on her face.

"I don't think they liked it, Caroline," she said to me.

"Sure we liked it," said Walter, who sauntered over from the water cooler. "It's a terrific way to think about an investment portfolio. In fact, most customers don't think about their portfolios at all. We don't encourage them to do that. Too many of us are stock jockeys and don't look at the Big Picture. And a lot of customers like it that way. That's why those guys didn't react ... But there are a couple of things you left out."

"Like what, Walt?" asked Kitt.

"Well, how much money do you invest in each season, for example? That's 'asset allocation.'"

"Well, this may sound silly," Kitt replied, "but it comes right from the old Caboodles: don't put any more than your age into the cold seasons, Fall — I mean Autumn — and Winter."

"What do you, or they, mean by that?" I asked.

"I mean, or rather, they meant, that if you are 45-years-old, don't put more than 45% of your investment money into income-producing, warm season stuff. As you grow older, you have less time to make a pile, less time to make money from growth stocks. But, to deal with inflation, you always have to have some of your investment dollars in growth stocks — even if you're 85-years-old."

By this time, I knew a rule when I heard one.

KITT & CABOODLE'S COMMANDMENTS

9. Income-producing investments (versus growth stock investments) should not be a higher percentage of the portfolio than your age.

"Too many people have too *much* income-producing stuff and not enough growth stuff. As I've said before, you buy shade trees that'll grow and give you shade, or fruit trees that don't grow very tall but give off fruit — or income."

"That's a few too many metaphors for me," said Walter. "But keep up the good work, Kitt. You've got a good idea there." He walked off, leaving me to contemplate Kitt's metaphorical orchard.

"This is what I mean," she explained. "Spring and Summer are the times when the economy is growing, right? Buy shade trees! Autumn and Winter are times of transition and no growth, OK: Buy fruit trees and live off the harvest! Got it?" She was now pleased with herself.

"Yeah, I think so. But explain the age thing again. I already wrote it down as a Rule, but I want to make sure I understand."

"Well, no *higher* a percentage of your portfolio than your age should go into the fruit trees. You're how old?"

"Uh, indeterminate age. Let's say forty-something," I mumbled.

"Okay, I'm thirty-something. Let's split the difference. No *more* than forty percent of the money for our joint portfolio should go into buying the Autumn or the Winter investments: Remember, those things that produce high income. Fruit.

"The rest should go into growth stocks. Shade trees. U.S. companies and international for Spring and Summer.

"And the Caboodles only said, 'No *higher* a percentage than your age.' There's no Caboodle rule saying you can't invest a smaller percentage than your age. They really liked shade trees better."

"So the money I still have in the money market fund and CDs is a Winter kind of investment?" I asked.

"NO," Kitt yelped. "Money market funds aren't investments at all! They're cash. Short-term CDs are cash, too. Just parking places."

"Why?" I still didn't quite get it. I sort of liked having ready money sitting in a money market fund.

Kitt explained: "Investments are like seeds that you plant in fertile ground. By themselves, seeds are pretty worthless. They are *supposed* to be planted and to grow. That's what your investment portfolio does for you, ideally. Of course, it's always possible that even planted seeds won't grow the way you want them to.

But keeping your investment money in cash is like scattering the seeds on top of the ground. Nothing happens to them. They just lay there. Or worse, they blow away."

"Well, what do we do with cash, then? I mean, you need to have *some*, don't you?" Not that I had much.

"Cash is outside of your investment portfolio, unless you sell something or if one of the Winter bonds matures. Then you put the money back to work in the same seasonal kind of investment. See?"

"I think so."

"I hope the other guys see it, too. It really worked for the Caboodles. Once someone's portfolio is all set up to cover each season, you don't have to sweat about what's happening in the market or with interest rates or politics. You're ready for just about anything. No trading stuff around. You don't have to be making decisions all the time."

"Okay," I said. "So what do we do with *our* money *now*?"

"Be patient," Kitt answered. "We're going to find the best quality REITs or utilities for Autumn and a good municipal bond mutual fund for our Winter money."

"So how do we do that?" I felt slow, dim-witted. Not unusual for me.

"There's good research on each one of those investments. We can consult with our own real estate analyst, as well as look at *Value Line* for ideas on REITs. For good utility research, Duff & Phelps is the best source. And Morningstar, which is the service that ranks mutual funds, includes municipal bond funds, too."

"What makes a good REIT?" I wondered aloud.

"Well, for one thing, it should own the real estate itself, not just the mortgages on the real estate. We like an 'equity' REIT … the other is

called a 'mortgage' REIT."

"Makes sense." I paused and then added, "I hate to admit this, but I'm not sure what a REIT really is."

"It's a way to raise money from a company's real estate. It's also a way for the real estate company to pass its revenues (at least 75% needs to be from the real estate) on to the shareholder and avoid paying taxes on them. If they do that, they can structure themselves as a REIT and get that tax benefit. Of course, the shareholder has to pay taxes on the income he or she receives."

"Of course," I murmured.

"There are all kinds of REITs. Some are dedicated to holding apartment complexes, some to industrial parks, others to shopping centers. Some REITs have a mixed-use kind of real estate in them.

"There are health-care REITs and hotel REITs. There are even racetrack REITs. But, to be considered good enough quality for us, a REIT would have to meet certain criteria: Proven management, location in a prosperous place for the kind of real estate it holds, and the cash flow to be able to raise its dividend regularly."

"How do we know if the cash is flowing fast enough to do that?"

"It'll be in any research report or company report, usually under the heading, 'cash from operations.' Cash flow is to REITs what earnings are to growth companies. It's a way to judge the REIT's growth potential. If the cash flow is growing, the dividend will be able to grow, too."

"There seem to be lots to choose from," I said, remembering a recent article in the newspaper about some local property being offered as a REIT.

"There sure are. It's a way for companies that hold a lot of real estate to raise money. And investors like REITs because they pay high dividends, compared to things like CDs and money market funds. At least, right now they do."

Kitt thought for a minute and then continued: "With all these new offerings, I worry about the quality. There are lots of really flaky REITs now, with poor management and poor cash flow.

"As a general rule, lower-quality REITs have to offer higher dividends to attract investors. That's one way to tell if the quality is considered high or low — if the dividend is relatively low or high.

"As another general rule (my own), I won't invest in a newly-formed REIT. We may miss some good deals by sticking with this rule, but I really want to see how well the management does and how well the cash flows before taking a chance. And I want to know that management holds some — not too much, but some — of the stock, too."

"What's not too much?" I asked.

"Oh, between 10% and 20% would be enough, I guess, to make sure they stay interested," Kitt answered.

"Okay by me, Chief."

Though we left together, I went back to my desk to type up the meeting notes for Mr. C and to ponder the Four Seasons, as they related to my financial future.

The McWeedies' Retirement Portfolio

Kitt began to market her Four-Season Portfolio Plan in earnest, starting with the McWeedies. Of course, by now she was always starting her work by asking Caboodle Questions:

- *Purpose*
- *Time horizon*
- *Amount of money available*
- *Risk tolerance*
- *And tax considerations for the money to be invested*

"I want the McWeedies to organize their thinking about their portfolio, Caroline. I think that a lot of people just buy stuff on impulse. No discipline. Going over these questions gets their attention," Kitt said.

Because the McWeedies were each 65-years-old and just starting their retirement, their time horizon was a little complicated.

"Retirement portfolios are both short-term and long-term," Kitt said. "They need income to live on now and growth for the long years ahead." So she devised a plan which put about 65% of the McWeedies' money into the income-producing side of their economic year — the Autumn and Winter seasons. Kitt advised them to put the remainder

into growth stocks, covering both Spring and Summer.

"But conservative, adult-type growth stocks, Caroline. They can't tolerate a lot of risk because they can't replace losses with salaries. We definitely don't want to force the McWeedies into becoming babysitters.

"As far as the Autumn and Winter are concerned, I'm buying the best quality utilities and equity REITs for them," she explained as she handed me several tickets. "And some triple-A-rated medium-term municipal bonds, too.

"You know, it's funny. Some people would rather do ANYTHING than pay taxes," Kitt said. "Sometimes they'd end up with more income after paying tax on bond interest than they would get from tax-free municipals, yet they STILL want the municipal bonds."

"It's the principal of the thing, I guess," I said.

"Not the principal, the interest. Heh. Heh," chuckled Kitt. Financial puns amused her.

"But how do you know if you'd get more income from tax-frees or taxable bonds?" I asked, ignoring the pun.

"It's easy if you have a calculator. Just divide the tax free percentage by the reciprocal of your tax bracket: That'll give you what's called the equivalent taxable yield."

"Okay, I'm in the 30% tax bracket. I subtract 30 from 100 and get 70. That's the reciprocal of my tax bracket, right?"

"Yup. If the tax-free bond is offering 5% yield, you divide 5 by 70 and come up with .714. So if you can get more than 7.14% in a taxable bond, you're better off with it than with the tax free municipal. You'll have more money left over after paying taxes than you'd get with the tax-free."

"So you're buying the McWeedies these bonds. When will they come due?"

"I'm 'laddering the maturities.' Do you know what that means?"

"Sure." A lot of brokers did this with bonds. They buy bonds that'll come due every five years or so. That way, customers will know they'll have cash coming back into the portfolio regularly. Then, if interest rates go up, they'll be able to increase their income by buying bonds with the higher rates.

"When long term rates are high, I'll buy more of the long-term bonds. If they're low, say, not much higher than what the medium-term

bonds are offering, then I'll buy more of the medium- and short-term bonds," Kitt said.

"But I'll *never* buy junky, low-quality bonds for the Four-Season Portfolio."

"How do you know what's good quality?" I asked. This was another thing I never understood and had felt too dimwitted to ask about.

"Well, in a bond, you can find out how Standard & Poor's and Moody's rate it. Along with the information on the common stock of a company, S&P issues credit ratings for bonds. So does Moody's.

"What they're doing is rating the bond issuer's ability to pay its bills. The bill you're most interested in getting paid is the interest on your bond.

"For a utility to be considered good quality, the payout ratio should be between 55% and 75%."

"Thanks, Kitt," I said, smiling. "That sure clears the whole thing up."

She laughed. "Oh, sorry about that. The payout ratio is how much of the earnings the utility pays to the shareholders. If it pays out all the earnings, it won't be possible for it to raise its dividend.

"And remember, you want the dividends to grow, at least equal to the rate of inflation, so that the McWeedies can keep up their purchasing power.

"Another thing to look at is the regulatory climate in the state. If it's *un*favorable, the utility will have a hard time raising rates to cover any rise in costs.

"Right now, utilities are changing. They aren't nearly as heavily regulated by the government as they used to be. So it's a good idea to check out what kind of 'de-regulated' business they're into, too." Kitt looked down at her notes and then up at me. "This sounds like a lot of stuff to do, but there's another thing that's good to know about utilities before buying them. Is your utility the high or low cost provider of utility services in the region it serves? See, big industrial companies can now shop around, and they can take their business elsewhere if they want to. So, finally, I guess, you need to know whether or not the utility you might buy has a lot of big industrial companies as customers."

"Well, for heaven's sake, where does somebody find this stuff out?" I asked.

"The best sources of utility information, *I* think, are Duff and Phelps and Argus. They publish research on utilities and answer all these questions. You can also find out a lot from *Value Line* and Standard & Poor's reports."

I nodded and said, "We ought to list these in our portfolio notebook, as a checklist for the future."

INVESTING IN HIGH QUALITY UTILITIES

1. ***Dividend Payout Ratio***
2. ***Regulatory Climate in State***
3. ***Non-regulated Businesses***
4. ***High or Low-Cost Provider in Region***
5. ***Customer Base***

"Good idea. We'll have a list for utilities and a list for REITs available for any additions we make to the Autumn portion of our portfolio."

"You said that convertible bonds could be used for Autumn, too. Explain those to me, if you've got the time, okay?

"Sure." She went on to explain that convertible bonds were like regular bonds, money that we lent to a company that would pay us interest twice a year and pay off completely at the bond's maturity date.

"But they also have a special feature to them — the 'equity-kicker.' We can convert the bonds into the common stock of the company, if we want to …"

"Why would we want to?" I asked.

"Because we think the stock is going to go up and we'll get more money for it than the money we lent the company in the first place plus interest. So with this equity kicker, our investment could also grow. You know, *grow* as in growth stocks."

"So, with convertible bonds, you get the interest and you get your money back, but you also might get growth?"

"Right, as long as you've bought really good convertible bonds and

have no fears that the company can't pay its interest or retire its debt when maturity date comes."

"So how much stock do we get for each bond?" I asked Kitt.

"Each bond has a conversion price — the price on the stock when you convert it from a bond. Knowing this, you come up with the conversion ratio, how many shares you get for converting."

"Give me an example, please." I thought I was getting it but wasn't sure.

"If the conversion price is 40 for a $1000 bond, then the conversion ratio is 25 because you'll get 25 shares at $40 to equal the face amount of the bond — what you paid for it when it first came out."

"And if the price of the company's stock is more than $40, what happens then?"

"Then the price of your $1000 bond goes up, too!" Kitt said. "That's the equity kicker. You get interest income, you get paid back at maturity if nothing happens to the company's stock, and you get growth potential, too, if the company's stock goes up. Because the bond price *will* go up."

"Sounds like such a good deal that we should have a whole portfolio of convertible bonds."

"It's hard to find that many really good ones. And the interest is always lower than regular bonds, because of the equity kicker. And most brokerage firms will require a minimum purchase of $5000.

"It's possible to buy convertible bond mutual funds, too. I'll check into it, look at some prospectuses to see if we want to do that. Maybe the McWeedies should have a mutual fund of convertible bonds as well," said Kitt as she walked over to the shelf where we kept the mutual fund prospectuses.

Mutual Funds

"Can't buy these things without doing your homework either, Caroline," she called to me, waving a sheaf of colorful brochures in her hand.

"Who would do such a thing?" I mused, knowing that most people haven't a clue as to how to do "homework" on mutual funds.

"A lot of people," Kitt answered earnestly. "Oh, you're kidding," she said when she saw my face. "Well, you're right. I guess it's difficult to know what to look for in these things."

"Right. All of them tell you how much money has been made in the past investing in that kind of fund." On slow days, I had taken to reading those brochures for amusement. I still didn't know anything.

"These brochures *aren't* prospectuses. See, they say right here on the bottom of the back page ..."

"In tiny print, for all to see ..."

"'Ask to see a prospectus before buying, and here" — she dug behind the pile to retrieve a limp booklet of small pale print — "is the prospectus."

"So what do we look for in that?" I asked again.

"Under fees," she said, flipping through the pages, "look for expense ratio. Here it is on page 32. Management fees, plus all other fees, come to 1.75% in this fund. That's okay. The average is between 1% and 1.8%, depending on what kind of a fund it is and how much management is required. You know, a fund of baby companies would have a lot more activity and, therefore, more management required. So you'd expect to pay a higher expense ratio.

"But a bond fund, where the manager just buys the bonds and lets them sit until maturity, doesn't need a lot of watching. Shouldn't have to pay much for management of that kind of fund."

"Those things are all load funds, aren't they?" After all the years I'd worked at Caboodle & Company, I *did* know about load and no-load mutual funds. Brokers don't sell the "no-load" variety. A "load" is the commission paid to the broker for selling the mutual fund.

"Right. Some have low loads, and some have no loads up front but charge an additional fee every year."

"How do I tell if that is happening?"

"It's called a 12-B-1 fee and is listed in the prospectus under fees."

"Makes sense."

"A load is only charged once. All the charges are clearly spelled out in here and should be checked carefully. Because high expenses just cut into the performance of the fund. Naturally."

"So I guess I'd better have a checklist for mutual funds, too. I know I'll forget it all if I don't write it down."

Kitt told me everything that a person should know about a mutual

fund before investing.

"These things can change over time. You know, managers leave and performance slips, but that sort of stuff doesn't hit the major newspapers." Kitt was rummaging through her papers and pulled out a sheet marked Morningstar. "This company — Morningstar — evaluates mutual funds and publishes the information. Good old *Value Line* does mutual fund evaluations, too. And they both update the information every quarter. You get all the information you need about a fund — even more than is in the prospectus."

"How do you get hold of one of those," I gestured to the sheet of paper she held.

"Caboodle & Company subscribes to it. A lot of brokerage firms do. Libraries usually have Morningstar and *Value Line* mutual fund reports, too. People can subscribe to them themselves, if they want to. It doesn't cost THAT much, a few hundred dollars a year. Which is still tax-deductible as an investment expense.

"Then they can get information on the funds that Caboodle & Company doesn't sell, like no-load funds."

"Bite your tongue," I said, knowing how the Caboodles had eschewed the no-load funds that didn't pay brokers for selling them. Kitt frowned.

"Yeah," she said. "Could be a problem."

CHAPTER SIX: WRESTLING WITH FUNDAMENTAL PROBLEMS

Kitt Has a Problem: The Broker's Paradox

That mutual fund discussion was early in the week. Later on, around Friday I think it was, I noticed that something was wrong with Kitt. She wasn't bubbling over like a glass of Kicky Kola the way she usually was. She came in early, as always, but barely glanced up at me or Mr. C when we arrived. She was reading her research, making her calls, putting in her tickets as usual, but the bounce was gone.

I didn't know what the problem was, but I did know this: Kitt couldn't keep it to herself for long. Sooner or later, she'd come out with whatever was bugging her — either to me or to Mr. C. (She rarely confided in the Royal Georges or the other brokers.)

"Those guys can't keep their mouths shut," she told me once. But she knew that telling me anything was like sealing it into a time capsule. I waited for her to disgorge. And sure enough, one day she asked me to have a cup of coffee with her, saying "I need to talk."

We sat in the employee's lounge, sipping coffee in silence while Kitt mulled potential wordings around in her head. Finally, she said, "Something is terribly wrong with this business. I know it and I don't know what to do about it."

"What do you mean?" I asked.

She went on as if I hadn't spoken. "It's so obvious and so pervasive. But I don't know what to do about it," she repeated, almost to herself. Then she looked up at me.

"Caroline."

"Kitt." I waited.

"The only way we brokers get paid is to buy or sell something in a customer's account."

I stared at her. And waited some more. *This* was the Big Problem?

"It isn't right." Kitt shook her head slowly and got up to refill her coffee cup. "I'm putting the Caboodles' Four-Season philosophy to work in my accounts. I think I've done a pretty good job of buying stocks and bonds that don't need to be replaced."

"I'm sure you have," I reassured her.

"But unless I find something to replace, I don't get paid. That isn't right."

She was beginning to see why the brokers hadn't embraced her Four-Season portfolio with much enthusiasm.

"Caboodle & Company would go out of business if we didn't make money on trades," I reminded her.

"I know. That's the big problem. That means that what's good for Caboodle is bad for my customers."

"Well, you need a lot of customers. Can't you just keep finding new ones to invest for?" I offered.

She laughed weakly. "That's like Basil making money by opening new units instead of raising its same-store sales."

"I see your point."

"It boils down to this: What I get paid for is finding things to buy or sell for commissions. It's hard to be honest with people. How can I say that all I want is to help them make enough money to retire, or to send their kids to college, when what I'm really doing is making money for ME to retire or to send MY kids to college?"

"You don't have kids," I said lamely.

"You know what I mean."

I did know what she meant. And I also knew that it was probably the real reason I had never become a broker. It's the paradox in the investment business: the only way a broker earns respect from the Company is by generating big commissions. The only way a broker earns respect from customers is by investing in good securities. By definition, the two are incompatible: good securities rarely need to be traded. In fact, it was our rule to sell *only* when "the reasons we bought the stock had changed or gone wrong" — as they had with Basil.

Kitt went on. "You know, I'm giving these talks to groups about how to invest and about the differences between stocks and bonds. That sort of thing.

"So when someone comes up to me and asks for help with their investments, I find myself looking at what they own and *always, always* suggesting that they make changes. Through me."

"Well, what's wrong with that? They're asking for your help."

"Because maybe what they already own isn't so bad," said Kitt, looking into the coffee cup and then up at me. "And I still tell them to sell."

Poor Kitt. She looked like she'd just confessed to murder. "But that's the business! That's what stockbrokers do for a living," I said.

"I rest my case," she replied.

"But you also tell your customers about having too much cash, and about having too many income-producing things, remember? The Four-Season Plan?"

"Yes, but do I go too far? Do I suggest changes that aren't necessary? Yes, sometimes I do, and it isn't right." Abruptly, Kitt stood up, nearly knocking over the table.

I was dismayed. "But you've got a good business going. It would be awful to quit now."

"I know. I have to figure out another way. There HAS to be a better way to do this work."

I stood up, too, and we walked out of the room together. En route, Kitt said, "I'll think of something."

"Don't quit," I implored her. "It would be so crushingly boring here without you. And I'd have to find another broker to trust."

Kitt finally got up the nerve to march into Mr. C's office and tell him of her Big Problem. When she came out, she looked excited and pleased. "I talked to him, Caroline. Told him just how I feel."

"So what did he say?" I asked, thinking, this should be interesting.

"Turns out he feels exactly the same way! He said to me, 'It's just like piecrust, Kitt.'"

"Huh?" I said.

"'If you play around with piecrust dough, it gets tough.' That's what he said." (Mr. C is an accomplished cook. Did I mention that?)

Kitt continued, "Then he said that managing a portfolio of stocks

gets tough if you mess with it too much. His father always told me, 'Set-it and forget-it, son. Get the right company to begin with and watch it grow.'"

"'But, Mr.C, how do we make commissions to live on if we do that?' I asked him."

"'I don't know, Missy. I never could figure it out,' he told me. He sounded pretty sad about it.

"Then I hit him with my idea, Caroline. 'Forget commissions,' I said. He almost choked. 'Charge a fee for just doing the right thing. Even if it means doing nothing.'"

"What did he say to that?" I asked.

"'Well, why does a customer need us if he isn't going to *do* anything with the money?'"

"Good answer."

"'They need us to tell them when to hold 'em, when to fold 'em ...'"

"'When to walk away, when to run,'" I sang. "Then what?"

"Then he said, 'Let me think about that' and he twirled his chair to look out his window."

"The think-pose," I said.

"Right. He's doing that now. He and I are going to figure out a way to charge customers for our expertise. That way, we can help them buy right and hold for as long as things are working out well, and we can find them new things to buy when things don't work out well. We'll be *advisers*, rather than just stock buyers and stock sellers."

"But what if the customers would rather pay the commissions? If they don't do anything for months, years at a time, they wouldn't want to pay a fee."

"True. We'd give them the choice. OH!" Kitt sighed, sitting down hard on her wooden desk chair. "I feel SO much better now."

Walter Turns Pro

The fee idea didn't strike everyone's fancy, but Walter Goodale liked it. "Too many of my decisions have been based on the need for commissions," he stated flatly to Kitt the day after she announced the new choice.

"Oh, I don't think I've made bad choices for my customers and they aren't unhappy. But I am. There are some stocks that I wish I hadn't sold and lots that I wish I hadn't bought. And I wouldn't have, if I hadn't had to make a living." He had the same look of relief that had been on Kitt's face when we talked in the coffee room. "Wow. This is going to be great."

Walter walked back to his desk and sat down. Then, abruptly, he stood and, carrying his account books, strode resolutely to my desk. "I'll be in the conference room," he told me, and marched away. This was not unusual behavior for Walter, who liked to work alone and away from the noise and distraction of the big front room.

Lots of brokerage firms have big rooms where all the brokers sit together, like ours. They're called "bullpens" — an unconscious acknowledgment of an all-male or mostly male sales force. All the hubbub is supposed to keep the level of idea generation high. It's assumed that the noise consists of fertile thoughts on how to make money instead of chat about the scores of last night's ball games. Some of the more senior brokers had little alcoves of their own where they and their customers could have more privacy, but not much more. When a broker wanted to be alone with a customer or with his (her) thoughts, there was the Dining Room, the Caboodle & Company version of a conference room.

Walter disappeared into the Dining Room and holed up there for the next couple of days. Finally, he emerged and walked over to Kitt's desk. "Kitt," he began, "I want to talk to you."

"Sure, Walt," she said. "What's up?"

"I've made a decision. Need your advice."

Kitt looked pleased. "Thanks, Walter." She put down the research report she was reading and asked, "Do you want to talk here?"

"Sure." I was glad of that because I could hear what was said firsthand instead of getting the re-run later.

"I've been thinking about this for a long time," Walter began. "And your idea of charging fees instead of commissions got me to re-examine my approach to this business. I'm really grateful for that."

Again, Kitt looked pleased. She smiled in encouragement and said nothing. We were both waiting for the punch line.

"I've decided to go out on my own. As a professional money manager." He looked closely at Kitt for her reaction. It was immediate.

"Gosh. Walter. That's ... that's great. But why? Can't you do the same thing as a stockbroker charging a fee?"

"Almost. I've been asking myself that for the past three days." He spoke quickly, earnestly. "But I want to manage money with complete independence — generate my own ideas, use research from a lot of different brokerage firms. This place is terrific and I've loved it here." Walter looked around. I concentrated on the papers on my desk before his gaze hit me. "But it's time for me to go out on my own," he concluded.

"Mr. C is going to be really upset at your leaving," Kitt said. She was certainly right. Walter was one of our most respected brokers and one of the few with solidly gray hair. His front room look of senior statesman enhanced our image, lending an air of sober respectability that was downright comforting to new customers coming through our doors for the first time.

"He'll be upset at my taking my customers with me," Walter said. "But I'll put the brokerage through you so he'll still get commissions on trades."

Walter meant that he'd call Kitt when he wanted to buy or sell securities in his managed accounts and she'd place the orders for him. Money managers don't usually do these transactions themselves, but call stockbrokers to "broker" the trades.

"Thanks, Walter. That's really nice of you."

"Of course, you'll have to give me a big discount," Walter laughed. Money managers charge their clients a fee, as well as pass along the costs of transactions. So most of them negotiate with brokerage firms (who do the actual buying and selling based on the money manager's recommendation) for deeply-discounted commissions, the tradeoff being that the orders are for large numbers of shares.

See, a money manager might want to buy, say, Mom's Mums, and put it into all the accounts he or she manages. So the order wouldn't be for a hundred shares or even a thousand shares, but maybe five thousand shares. There'd be big commissions, so the money manager would want a really big quantity discount.

I knew this because Kitt did business with other professional managers, and she'd explained it to me. These pro money managers look for pots of investment money to manage that are huge: over a million dol-

lars is the usual minimum. (Most of them prefer over five million.) Oh, sure, some work with less, say $250,000, but they can't make any money without charging a minimum annual fee, usually between $4000 and $5000. Such fees take such a big chunk out of their smaller-sized pots that investors decide it isn't worth it to retain a money manager.

Money managers' *clients* (somehow going from stockbrokers to money managers turns these people from "customers" into "clients") are rich people who've earned a lot of money and don't know what to do with it, or people who've just inherited a big sum or received a large settlement of money on something. Or the client could be a college's endowment fund or a company's pension plan.

Mostly these people go to professional money managers because they think they'll get more objective advice and more personal attention than they would from stockbrokers. Also, when there's a lot of money at stake for an organization, like a school system's or a company's pension plan, it's presumed that the professional money manager is more prudent and objective. Boards of directors, people with a fiduciary responsibility, prefer to pay the manager's fee for advice, rather than the commissions of a stockbroker who makes all his money by buying and selling.

Anyway, with the million dollar minimum investment for each client account, the manager can diversify over a lot of different stocks, often as many as 35, with sufficient numbers of shares in each.

"I plan to manage individual accounts with a minimum of $250,000 to begin with, and I'll only charge a $3750 minimum fee," Walter said with excitement in his voice. "Eventually, I'll pool the small accounts (he meant, manage them all as if they were one) and do the individual management of accounts over $5 million. Maybe even start a small mutual fund." His voice took on a dreamy quality. Both Kitt and I could tell that Walter had already left us.

Money managers, like bank trust departments, sometimes "pool" small accounts and manage them as if they were one, the way Walter suggested. There's nothing wrong with this, as long as clients understand that their accounts will no longer be managed individually.

Walter sped on, "Once I have a decent track record and enough money to manage, I'll get in touch with the professional consultants, get them to put me on their databases and find clients for me."

In the money management world, there are professional consultants who spend their days interviewing prospective money managers for their clients. They keep large databases of information about each manager's investment style and performance record, how much money they manage, and how many people work for them, along with lots of other details.

These consultants then try to match the managers with their clients, who have many millions to invest and don't have the time or energy to search out managers themselves — clients such as pension fund advisers, state retirement plans, or the just plain ultra-rich.

"I'll use Caboodle & Company to clear for me," Walter went on. Money managers need to have the same kind of back-office operations that brokerage firms do. But most are too small to have their own, so they hook up with a larger firm and use theirs — for a price, of course. These larger firms are "clearing" the trades and other regulated operations for the little firm. Caboodle & Company did that for a lot of managers and also for some very small brokerage firms. It was a profitable business and had helped make up some revenues we lost when all our brokers left for National.

"It sounds like you've made up your mind, Walt," Kitt said. "You said you needed my advice. On what?"

"I really just wanted to tell someone," Walter laughed. "To practice before I broke it to Caboodle."

"Well, thanks for choosing *me*," said Kitt, standing and holding out her hand. "Good luck. I'll enjoy working with you as your broker."

Walter flushed, his cheeks rosy with excitement. He looked like a gray-haired boy as he stood and strode into Mr. C's office.

Joe and the Wrap Account

The fee versus commission debate not only inspired Walter with thoughts of career moves, but piqued Joe's interest as well. Joe was Kitt's first "recruit" to Caboodle & Company back in the days just before Mom's went public. As soon as Kitt suggested charging a fee instead of commissions, he started talking about becoming a "consultant" to his customers. It seems that Joe was beginning to lose some of his larger accounts to professional money managers.

"It happens when an account gets to about $500,000," he told Kitt. "All of a sudden, they tell me they need someone who charges a fee, not a commission."

Kitt told Joe about Walter's plans. "Good idea," Joe commented. "Walter will be good at that. He's got good ideas and he likes to do a lot of research on his own." Joe moved some papers from the chair next to Kitt's desk onto the floor and sat down. "But I like to talk with customers, I like to meet new people all the time. That's really more up my alley than managing money. I think consulting would be fun."

He told Kitt that he would ask those customers who wanted to move their money to a money manager if he could have the job of finding an appropriate person to do the job. He would charge a fee for this — some annual percentage of the assets in the account. Then he would monitor the manager's performance to make sure that he/she was doing the best for the client.

"Some of these customers have accounts that eventually have more than one manager. I could help them find those and watch over them once they're hired."

"But the customer would have to pay two fees then — one to you and one to the money manager."

"Well, we'd wrap it all up into one fee. Other brokerage firms are doing this and they call it a wrap account. The business stays with Caboodle, the fee wraps around all the services: finding the money managers, the money manager's fee, the transaction costs, and my fee. One fee covers everything. Sort of like one-stop shopping."

"Sounds expensive," said Kitt, who looked dubious.

"Well, isn't that what the professional consultants do?" Joe asked, defensively.

"Sure," Kitt replied. "But they don't sell stocks, too. They do a lot of work, checking up on each money manager personally and keeping those huge databases of information that they update quarterly.

"And they know a lot about how to evaluate money managers. If the manager's performance was terrific or terrible, or somewhere in between, the consultant knows how it got there. It's a lot of work, Joe."

Joe ignored her tone and went on. "With smaller customers, I can shop around for mutual funds — I could even buy no-load funds and charge a fee for investing in the best of those. I figure it could be one and a half, maybe two percent. Some firms are charging as much as three percent of the assets in wrap fees. Then they put customers into no-load mutual funds. The idea is to switch into other funds when the time is right."

"As soon as you charge a fee for no-load funds, they become load funds. How do you explain *that* to a customer?" asked Kitt, who didn't seem to like this idea much.

"There are thousands of funds for people to choose from. Customers might rather have me make the choice for them. Saves them time, research, uncertainty, stuff like that."

"I guess that's true. But how will you know when to switch or even *if* to switch people from one fund to another?" Kitt looked at Joe intently.

"There are services that I can subscribe to that do the timing. Or I can listen to our analysts and decide for myself."

"I've seen a lot of research studies on this mutual fund switching idea. That kind of market-timing just hasn't worked consistently well, Joe," said Kitt.

"Well, I wouldn't switch often. Maybe not at all."

"Then why would anyone pay a fee for you to do what they could have done free — buy no-load mutual funds? Or pay a fee every year for what you do in year one only?"

"For my charm." He got up abruptly, and sounded annoyed at her lack of enthusiasm. "Lots of firms are doing this, you know," he said a little querulously. "Caboodle & Company should get on the bandwagon. Wrap accounts are the latest thing. The customers love them."

"That's because they don't understand how expensive these wrap accounts are. I think it's better to tell them the truth and, without charging a fee, advise them on which fund would be best. That's what we've always done."

"We've *never* recommended no-loads," said Joe, his voice rising.

"That's true," Kitt conceded.

"And I don't see how this is any different than what you're doing, charging a fee instead of commission to manage a customer's account."

"Because it is for the *whole account.* And it's much less than what you're talking about. An additional one and a half to 2% or more of a person's investment portfolio is a lot of money, when you deduct it from the assets year in and year out. With your fees added to the manager's fees, it could cost a customer 3% or more a year. That's just too much.

"And I don't believe in switching funds, in this market-timing stuff." Kitt pawed through her notes and papers and pulled out a graph. "Look at this graph of the stock market. Standard & Poor's index of 500 companies' stocks has gone up dramatically over the fifty years that records have been kept.

"It's clear to me that the only strategy that's worked consistently is to buy good quality investments and hold them over time. You sell ONLY when something goes wrong with the investment or your own needs change."

Kitt leaned forward in her chair and asked, "Why not offer to find the right money manager for your larger accounts, for a small charge or even no charge? Then the money manager will put the trades that he or she makes through you here at Caboodle & Company."

Joe looked doubtful. "Then all I get is the commissions on deeply discounted trades. Most money managers won't do business with you unless you give big discounts."

"True. And they shouldn't. It costs the customer too much and hurts the managers' overall performance."

"And what about those people who don't have the minimum for a money manager? The ones who just want no-load mutual funds? I can't make any money off them unless I charge a fee for finding and switching the funds." He stood up and said, "Caboodle & Company AND Joe aren't in the charity business. I gotta make a living, Kitt." And he walked away.

Kitt sighed. It was the same old paradox. Too many times, the right thing for the customer wasn't the right thing for the broker. She looked once more at the graph and then up at me. It was an argument that she'd have over and over again in the years ahead.

Who's In Charge Here?

"There are so many ways that customers can get professional help in managing their money these days, Caroline," Kitt said to me later. We were sitting at the table in the employee lounge, looking over our joint account and trying to decide what, if anything, we would add or subtract. It was our usual "quarterly review."

After the Joe incident, I'd asked Kitt to tell me more about money management advisers. First of all, everybody seemed to be doing it in one form or another these days. And second, I wanted to be able to pass it on to my aunt. She had all the money in our family — and had it all at a local bank, deposited there "just for the time being," she kept telling me.

"First, for the large accounts — those with half a million to a million dollars or more in investable assets — there's the professional money manager, like Walter. He or she will charge a fee based on a sliding scale, usually one percent at $1 million, plus transaction charges (what it costs to buy and sell the investments, though those should be deeply discounted).

"Then you have bank trust departments. Over the years, these guys haven't been known for good performance, although," she conceded, "there *are* some exceptions."

"And they drive you crazy with little charges all the time," I interjected. "My aunt has an account in the trust department of that bank down the street. They charge her for everything."

"Annoying, but it probably ends up being about 1%, even adding up all those irritating little costs," Kitt said. "The worst thing about trust departments is that they don't *usually* manage the money very effectively."

"So a customer who's rich can get money management advice from a money manager."

"If they turn over at least the minimum and let the money manager make all the investment decisions," Kitt said.

"Or they can buy mutual funds and get into the pool with millions of other people buying the same kind of stock or bond. That's another way to get professional money management for a fee."

"Or they can go to a bank trust department …" I was listing these things to try to keep them all straight.

"Right. Or there are a bunch of other individuals willing to give advice for a price. The ones with initials after their names."

"Like CFP? One of those has been calling my aunt on the phone."

"Right. The initials stand for Certified Financial Planner. Usually somebody from the insurance business. The idea here is to ask how the CFP makes his or her money. Make sure the person isn't just pushing a product. Better to get one of those CFPs who charges only a fee, and doesn't sell any products to go with the plan. Otherwise, you may find that the plan leans very heavily toward the product he sells — insurance, or stocks and bonds.

"If it's stocks and bonds that you want, it's best, I think, to go to the people who make it their primary business."

"What about those RIAs — Registered Investment Advisers?" I asked. Lots of brokers were taking the exam to get those particular initials.

"Doesn't mean much of anything. Just satisfies the federal regulators who keep a record of your name, address, that sort of thing. If a state requires an exam, it's usually a pretty easy one. I know," she said, "because I had an exam to take in order to do this fee-based management thing. But it doesn't insure the customer that I know anything much about investment advice. Just that I do it and the Feds *know* I do it."

"What about CLUs and CHFCs?" Talk about alphabet soup.

"Those are insurance industry initials, meaning Chartered Life Underwriter and Chartered Financial Counselor." Kitt got up to pour herself another cup of coffee. "Those guys have to take national exams that are really tough. I mean, really tough. My insurance salesman cousin in California showed me his books and I was *impressed.* But, once again, they're insurance people whose basic business is insurance, not investments."

"And then there are brokers," I said. "I wonder why there aren't any initials that tell people you're a broker."

"Like RR for Registered Representative, or FC, for Financial Counselor, or IR for Investment Representative?" Kitt laughed. "You know, each company has a title for brokers that says just about anything but 'stockbroker.' I've never been able to figure that out. A stockbroker by any other name is still a stockbroker. And nothing to be ashamed about,"

she said.

"I guess you all don't want to be called SBs."

"Might be misunderstood," Kitt replied.

"So how does a person like my aunt choose which of these experts to go to?"

"If she doesn't want to make the investment decisions, she should buy a mutual fund — after doing the homework to decide which one to buy, of course."

"Of course," I intoned.

"Or, if she has enough money, she could use a professional money manager whose style of investing she feels comfortable with."

I consulted my list. "Or she could stay with the bank trust department. I don't think she wants to do that."

"If she does want to make the final decisions — after getting advice — she could go to a broker who charges an annual fee with low commissions, like me," Kitt said, "or a broker who charges commissions for each trade — as long as she understands and approves each trade and doesn't get 'churned.'"

"Meaning the broker makes a lot of trades to make money for himself, not her."

"Right. The ever-present temptation: The broker's paradox."

"What about all those investment letters? My aunt keeps getting those things in the mail that promise to make her rich. How good are they?"

"I'd definitely avoid anything or anyone that *promised* to make her rich. And a person doesn't have to know *anything* to write an investment letter.

"That's not to say that there aren't some letters out there that are interesting to read, and have some good ideas about investing. But that's all they can offer: Ideas."

"So what do I tell my aunt?" I asked, knowing I'd get a straight answer from Kitt.

"Well," she thought for a minute before replying. "I guess I'd have to say that your aunt had better learn enough about investing to know what questions to ask. She can turn the investment decisions over to someone else, but she'll have to make the initial decision about who that someone

is. And to do that ..."

I completed the sentence for her, "... she'll have to do her homework." Can't get around that, I guess.

CHAPTER SEVEN: DOING HOMEWORK

MANAGING THE 401-K PLAN

Kitt and Mona of "Mom's Mum's" continued to be good friends. Kitt stopped by the farm often and Mona came into town occasionally for lunch. It was through this friendship that Kitt's business took a giant step forward.

One afternoon, Kitt appeared at my desk with a sheaf of papers in her hand and laid them in front of me. I looked at them and saw that they were new account forms for Mona Malloy — personal account, children's accounts, "Mom's Mum's" business account.

"Wow!" I said. "Good for you! This must be huge."

"Yeah," Kitt replied. "It's big."

"How'd you get the accounts?" I asked, knowing that Mona had been pursued by every broker in the state since Mom's Mums went public. Selling 55% of her company had netted her many millions of dollars which, of course, needed to be invested in something other than seed.

"She's had her accounts at National ever since she took the company public." I knew that. It had been considered a major failure when Caboodle & Company didn't "capture the assets" after the Mom's Mums offering. (That terminology, which sounds a lot like battleground talk to me, is actually used.) "Capturing the assets" means a broker at Caboodle would be able to manage the money that Mona personally got from going public.

But Mona had given her millions to an older guy at National, Caboodle's rival brokerage firm in town. He was a gray-haired smoothie who'd been around for years.

"So what happened?" I asked.

"Nothing. The broker was pretty good. He didn't lose any of the

money. But he was sort of arrogant, I guess. I don't know, really. He did a lot of trading in the account. She was never sure why."

"Huh," I snorted. "Try 'churning the account to get commissions.'"

"Well, I didn't want to say that. He's supposed to be pretty good. But when I told her about my Four-Season Portfolio Plan and that I was now charging a quarterly fee instead of commissions, she really liked the idea. She says she wants to try it out."

"Try it out? Looks like she's committed the whole family and the business to you, too." I thumbed through the account forms.

"Yeah." Kitt looked pleased. "She likes the idea."

"Big-time," I suggested.

"Big-time," Kitt agreed.

As I picked out the new report form that was second-from-the-top, I asked, "Who's Emma?"

"She's the daughter who lives out of town. Works in Philadelphia. That account won't have much in it. But Mom wants me to talk to her company about their 401-K plan."

A 401-K plan is a sort of company-IRA. A person's company will offer a plan that allows her to set aside money out of her salary for retirement — up to a certain amount — before it's subject to taxes. She must invest it in the choices offered to her. Usually there are several mutual funds from one "family" — that is, one investment company offering a bunch of different mutual funds.

We employees have a 401-K plan at Caboodle & Company and we get to choose from stock funds, bond funds, and/or money market funds. You can divide the money between as many funds as you want, as long as they're part of the mutual fund family that Caboodle has chosen. The brokers have been trying to get Caboodle to add an international mutual fund to the fund choices, so there's been a lot of talk about our 401-K lately.

Caboodle & Company used to offer its employees a retirement plan — called a profit-sharing plan. Unfortunately, company profits were so ridiculously small for a few years "BK" ("Before Kitt") that the employees would have had to work until they were about 120 years old before they took in any meaningful amount. That's when Mr. C decided to turn the whole thing over to the mutual fund company. Now Caboodle &

Company contributes a little bit each year, but it's really the employees who are building their own nest eggs.

People can take money out of their 401-K plans for emergencies without the IRS jumping all over them, too. That's not such a good deal, according to Kitt. "Too tempting for some people. This is the only retirement money a lot of people will have, except for Social Security.

"Not only that, but too many people aren't investing this money in common stocks. They're putting it into money market funds or bond funds. They won't have a prayer of making enough to live on in retirement," Kitt had said. She got real agitated whenever the subject of 401-K plans came up.

Looking at the new account form for Emma, Mom's daughter in Philadelphia, I asked Kitt what she planned to do for her.

"Mona is giving each of the kids $10,000. She plans to do that every year as long as she can. You know, she can give that much without their paying any gift tax on it." I nodded.

"But what are you going to invest it in? For Emma, I mean. She's got the 401-K. Can you put the $10,000 into that?"

"No. The company deducts money from her salary for that. But how she invests it *does* make a difference to what I do with this," she said, holding up a check that accompanied the account form.

"Why?" I asked.

"Because you have to look at your investments as one pot of money you're building for future use. I don't want to invest this check in aggressive growth stocks if she's already doing that in her 401-K plan. Remember the Four-Season Portfolio? The Caboodle Key is to diversify."

"I can see that. But what *should* Emma be investing in her 401-K plan?" I wondered because I have one, too. "What do you do with yours?"

"Oh, I put the Autumn and Winter stuff — you know, income producers — into my 401-K."

"Like the REITs and utilities, you mean."

"Right. I have a mutual fund that specializes in telephone utilities and holds some REITs, too. I also have a convertible bond mutual fund.

"And I have an IRA, too. I know it's not after-tax money, but it grows tax-deferred. So I use it for zero-coupon bonds."

"Hey, before you go on, tell me more about zero-coupon bonds. I've always wondered about those things. I know they don't pay any interest. Why would anyone buy them?"

"True, the so-called coupon or interest is zero. But you pay only a fraction of the face value for the bond. See, the interest is reinvesting and compounding itself for you. I think zero-coupons are great. You know, interest checks on regular bonds can be pretty paltry and people just fritter the money away unless there's something to reinvest it in. Well, you get around that problem by NOT getting the interest at all. For example, you can buy a zero-coupon treasury bond due in ten years and pay, say, $4000 for something that will give you $10,000 when it matures, because the interest is being reinvested in the bond.

"Of course, what you pay when you buy it depends upon the current interest rates. But it's always considerably less than the face (or maturity) value of the bond."

Kitt smiled as if delighted by this idea and then added, "But, you also have to remember that if you own zero-coupon treasuries or corporate bonds *outside* of a retirement plan, then you have to pay federal tax on the income even if you aren't actually receiving it."

I asked, "But if you buy bonds and keep them in the 401-K plan or the IRA, you pay no tax on the income?"

"Not until you take it out at age 59 and 1/2 or later."

"Years and years from now," I smiled.

"Right. And it makes some sense to have really aggressive growth stock funds in a tax-sheltered plan like the 401-K, too, if you're going to have them at all. So that you don't get socked with a lot of capital gains taxes."

It depressed me to recall that, according to the IRS, money you made on selling securities for a gain (thus a "capital gain") was taxed at the same level as your income.

"Do you think Emma should have the really aggressive growth stock fund?" I asked. "They're made up of baby-type companies, right?"

"If anyone should, she should. She's young. She has years to make up any losses, if they occur. But I need to check out some things in the prospectus that Mona gave me for that fund. You don't just pop money into any old fund just because it *calls* itself aggressive growth or whatever. You have to do your homework on mutual funds, too."

"Of course," I sighed. "There's *always* homework."

Reading Annual Reports

One day I commented to Kitt about the mountain of mail I was receiving in the name of our joint investment account. Kitt had used my home address on the account form, so I was getting everything sent to shareholders. At first, I brought it all into the office, but as we got busier at Caboodle & Company, and Kitt seemed always to have more than enough junk on her desk, I began to just toss it all in the wastebasket at home. Nothing looked that important. Of course, I kept monthly statements, but the other stuff — all those shiny books and voting things — looked too boring for words, so I pitched them immediately.

You should have heard Kitt when I told her *that.* She was shocked, to put it gently.

"You do *what*?" she asked with both disappointment and disbelief in her voice.

"Toss it?" I repeated. "It didn't look all that important to me."

Kitt passed a hand over her forehead and then said, "Remember the 'Know your company' rule of the Caboodles? How are you going to know the company if you don't read its letters?"

"*You'll* tell me?" I offered weakly.

"How am *I* supposed to know? You remember the Basil story. Maybe our analysts can't tell or won't tell or don't know everything to tell about our companies. They're *our* companies now. We have to take responsibility for at least reading the reports our companies send us."

Chastened, I replied, "Those things look so shiny, just like the mutual fund company brochures. Aren't they just hype ... just sales pieces?"

"Not really. Think of it this way: Those shiny annual company reports are a lot like the letters I used to write my folks from college. I'd start out with how well things were going. All the good news right up front, good grades, things like that.

"Well, that's what the president does with his opening message or letter. It's usually the first part of the annual reports, and it tells all the good news, like how much profits have grown and what new markets the company is going into. And if there's bad news to tell, it's going to come out in this part, too. Just like I eventually told my folks about my bad grades. (I remember being so mad when I got a "C" in BOWLING.) I may have had a lot of fancy explanations, and I would tell them eventually. Well, the president of the company does the same thing. So read that President's Message and you'll know about the good news, the bad news, and other assorted things about the company that you own.

"The next part, which is usually about the different businesses a company is in, has a lot of pictures in it. It's good to read this part, too, especially *before* you buy the stock. But look through it after you own it, too. It's important to know the businesses that a company is in.

"When I went away to college, my folks gave me a camera. I would send them photos that I'd taken of my college friends. That's what this section is like. Of course, in annual reports, the workers in the pictures are all happy, smiling, and culturally diverse. People that *everyone* can identify with. This middle section is usually put together by the company's marketing department.

"The last part of the annual report has all the numbers backing up the president's letter. The footnotes will explain anything unusual.

"It doesn't really take very long to read these things," Kitt chided. "You OWN companies now, Caroline. I own them, too, so I should've been asking you to show me the mail. We'll have to start reading the reports they send.

"Remember the reasons we wrote down for owning each company's stock? To see if we still want to own them, we need to check the annual and quarterly reports. That's one of the best ways to find out if those reasons are still valid. If they aren't — say, we find out that Mom's Mums is going into the car rental business or something — we'll probably want to sell the stock. And how would we know to do that if we didn't read the reports?"

"Well ..." I began.

"I know, I know," Kitt continued. "We'll know about Mom's because we know Mona. But we don't know the management of Kicky Kola. And this portfolio is going to own a lot of different stocks whose owners we don't personally know."

I held up my hand. "Enough said. I promise to read all the mail."

"And bring it in so I can read it, too, okay?"

"Right. I'll think of them as letters from my kids at college ... if I had kids."

"You want to know for yourself what your companies are doing, right?"

"Right."

"After all, reports come only once a quarter. The annual report is the biggest and most out-of-date, but read it anyway, especially *before* we buy the stock — so that we know exactly what the company's business is.

"The quarterly reports are short. They only take a few minutes to read. The proxy statements give a lot of personal information about the management.

"I don't mean to sound bossy about this, but I think you'll find this investment business much more interesting if you read the reports yourself. I'll read them, too. I promise. Then we can talk about them together."

Kitt smiled and added, "Mona said that her annual reports cost her a fortune and take forever to put together. She would definitely be upset if we didn't read them." Kitt laughed. "She hates the proxy statements, though. They tell her age AND her salary."

I thought about this for a minute and then asked, "Can't I get all this information just from *Value Line*?"

"It's a good idea to read both. You know, get the company's side of things and then see how *Value Line* perceives it. The more we know about our companies, the better."

"So how often does *Value Line* change their reports?" I was thinking about the time I would have to devote to this education.

"They run on a cycle, changing every quarter. You can stash all of it in a shoebox if you want, and we'll look at it every three months. It'll all come at about the same time and shouldn't take us more than an hour or so to read."

I can handle that, I thought. I had envisioned hours hunkered over research documents, reports, analyses. An hour or two spent each quarter with the easy-to-read *Value Lines* and the letter-home-type Annuals and Quarterlies suddenly sounded a lot better to me.

KITT & CABOODLE'S COMMANDMENTS

10. If you find yourself NOT reading your investment mail, put it in a shoebox for safekeeping. Then schedule two hours every three months to read all recent company and research reports on your investments.

CHAPTER EIGHT: CRISIS

TROUBLE AT CABOODLE & COMPANY

The month that Kitt celebrated her sixth year at Caboodle & Company, Mr. C became distracted by a huge problem that threatened to curdle Caboodle into an also-ran after nearly 80 years as an investment banking firm.

One day, Mr. C arrived at work the same time I did, tugging open the huge front doors to find Kitt already there.

"You got a call already, Mr. C. Message on your desk," she said, looking up from her work. "He said it's important."

"Okay. Who could it be at this hour?" It was just after seven a.m.

"I dunno. Sounded like David." David was the head trader for Caboodle's fixed income department.

Now, the fixed income department was rarely heard from at Caboodle & Company. "Fixed income" means bonds, not stocks — money that's lent to someone and that collects a stated amount of interest (hence, the name "fixed income") until it matures.

Fixed income stuff was pretty boring to most of the Caboodle & Company brokers and especially to Mr. C. The commissions paid for buying and selling bonds for customers was very close to nothing, which may have explained the lack of allure for brokers. And Mr. C just couldn't get excited about something in which he didn't have an ownership interest, the way stocks do. His Caboodle forebears all got rich owning companies (that is, owning STOCK in companies), not *lending* money to them.

Anyway, Mr. C disappeared into his office, but I heard him pick up his phone to call this guy David. He tried for hearty cheerfulness, but his voice cracked, unused to being activated at 7 a.m. "So, David! What's up

this early in the morning?"

David's answer caused Mr. C to cross the room and close his door. But, before he did, from my vantage point behind the reception desk, I could see his brow furrowing, and I wondered what was up.

We didn't find out right away. About 8:30 that morning, a couple of the executive committee guys arrived and closeted themselves with Mr. C, who came out once and said, grimly, "Please hold all calls, Caroline."

The brokers, taking note of this unusual pow-wow, gathered around Kitt's desk and began asking questions of her and of me.

"What's going on?"

"Wasn't that the head of the banking division?"

"What's the head of research doing here?" Even the Royal Georges deigned to be perplexed. All Kitt could say was that David the Trader had called Mr. C early that morning.

"Uh-oh," said the Georges in unison.

"Why uh-oh?" asked Kitt.

"Problems with bond trading ... could be expensive," one George answered, I'm not sure which. I have a hard time telling them apart.

Well, whichever one it was, he was right. That was a long and dark day in Caboodle history, deeply depressing to all of us who depended on the company for our livelihoods. First came the meeting behind Mr. C's closed door, then came David the Trader with another fellow in tow. He turned out to be a trader, too.

What traders do is to sit at desks upstairs, staring at machines that quote prices from other companies that buy and sell the same things they do — stocks, if they're stock traders, and bonds if they're bond traders. Anyway, they also have phones growing in their ears.

The bond traders will buy a bunch of bonds in order to turn around and sell them to somebody at a higher price or "mark-up." It's a lot like a store. You've got this inventory, you mark it up, and you move it out the door. Except that in the bond trading business, you've got to move it fast. Nobody likes to keep inventory overnight because the prices change so quickly and a lot of money can be lost if interest rates go up even a little bit.

Anyway, Mr. C's office was crowded with all those dour looking guys, the door was shut, and no one came out for hours. And nobody outside

the office left their desks. All of us pretended to work while straining our ears for hints about what was going on.

At one point, the murmur turned to a hum and then to angry barks. We looked at each other in alarm, Kitt and I: No one ever raised a voice here at Caboodle & Company.

After the door finally opened and the grim group dispersed, its members marching with lowered heads through the front room to the elevator or the door, Mr. C looked out at us with a stunned expression, as if surprised we were still there. Then he returned to his desk. Through the open door, I could see him holding his head in his hands.

The phone rang on one of the Georges' desks. He picked it up and said, "Caboodle & Company, George Cutter here." The ensuing conversation went something like this:

"Yeah, hi, Arthur … No, I haven't read it yet." George looked up, put his hand over the receiver and stage-whispered, "Anyone got a *Journal*?"

The other George reached under his desk and picked up the morning *Wall Street Journal*. He stood at his desk and tossed it onto George Cutter's.

"Page 12? Page twelve … column four … yeah, yeah, I got it. Yeah. Thanks, Art. Yeah, I'll call you." He hung up.

All of us, like a kind of chorus line, reached for our *Journals* — from wastebaskets, briefcases, the tops of desks. We turned in unison to page twelve and column four. And there it was: "Rumors Fly About Trading Loss At Caboodle & Company."

And underneath the headline appeared this brief story:

"Sources close to Caboodle & Company, the regional investment banking firm, say that trading losses in the bond department might be the largest in Caboodle history."

The story went on to relate a tale, unconfirmed but whispered about on the Street, of bond-trading ineptitude.

The article was horrible and, as it turned out, true. David the Trader had apparently made several huge and undetected interest rate bets — betting, that is, that the rates would NOT go up. Unfortunately, rates *had* gone up a lot recently and David's mistake now had to be paid off, at an enormous cost to Caboodle's capital.

Later, in a meeting, Mr. C confirmed this to all of the Caboodle employees. "I'm sorry that you had to read about this in the paper first. I don't know how the *Journal* got hold of the story before, well, before I even knew . . ." His voice trailed off.

A day or two later, a clerk in the trading department quit her job without explanation. I heard she was angry about not getting a raise, and that she'd been around when the mistakes by David the Trader were discovered. We put two and two together, speculating that, probably for revenge, she'd leaked the information about the mess-up to the *Journal*.

"What's going to happen to Caboodle & Company?" asked the Georges. "Is there enough capital to cover this loss?"

These boys were nothing if not direct. "Our customers have been calling," one explained.

"Yes, yes," replied Mr. C. He didn't sound confident. In fact, he sounded beaten.

What happened next became part of the company legend — one of those stories that old-timers tell to new hires when they try to explain the culture of the place.

During this siege, which is the only way I can describe the atmosphere, a slew of serious-looking Wall Street suits frequently came and went through our big front room. According to Kitt, the Royals knew some of them as deep-pockets from New York, senior people from other firms interested in taking over our company.

Others were Caboodles, heirs to the family fortune who appeared from their country estates and conferred with Mr. C while their drivers stood at attention next to shiny autos outside our big front door.

Meanwhile, the brokers continued calling customers, reading research, and holding sales meetings — to the outsider, carrying on business as usual. But Kitt knew differently.

"The Royals have been talking with other firms. Wouldn't it be just like them to jump ship at a time like this?" she whispered to me one afternoon. She handed me a ticket to buy 1800 shares of AT&T for one of her customers. "Here . . ." It was a huge buy for Kitt. I wondered if she'd made a mistake.

"1800 shares? Is that right?" I asked, looking at the name on the ticket. It was for somebody named Eleanor Kitt.

"Yeah. My aunt Ellie. She's my dad's sister. I don't get to see her much

'cause she lives in New York. But, right now, Aunt Ellie's in town for a couple of weeks. I just got her to transfer her account over to us."

I remembered the papers that Kitt had put on my desk that morning. Her face looked grim, as she added, "I hope we stay in business long enough to make it worth the paperwork."

"Does she know about the loss?"

"Oh sure. She knows everything. Aunt Ellie is a big investor. She reads the *Journal* from cover to cover, and the *Investors' Business Daily*, too. She doesn't hold Mr. C in terribly high regard, I'm afraid. Says she knew Caboodle & Company years ago, before Mr. C took over, that it was a great little company back then. Says Mr. C is a dilettante."

"That's a little harsh, don't you think?" Poor Mr. C. He tried his best. But I had to admit that he was a pretty dim bulb compared to his forebears. Those guys were legendary on Wall Street.

"Well, Aunt Ellie *is* harsh," said Kitt matter-of-factly as she walked back to her desk.

So here's what happened next. One morning soon after this, I was working my way through some posting. That means registering customer trades in the brokers' customer books (it's all done by computer now, but back then, we wrote down every trade by hand). Things had been very slow, and I was thinking about the implications of *that* just as Mr. C appeared in his doorway.

"I have an appointment arriving soon, Caroline," he said, his eyes on the huge front doors, which were open for business now that it was 8:30 a.m. He ran his fingers through where his hair would've been if it hadn't been sliding down the back of his head, spreading out like a skirt halfway down his scalp. This habit of running fingers over scalp must have been left over from earlier, hairier days. When he was worried or anxious, he did it a lot. It was then that his scalp became polished and shiny. That morning, it shone like an apple.

"Not to worry. I'll send him in," I told him, returning to my posting job.

"Him's a her. I mean, my appointment is female. Kitt's aunt Eleanor is coming in to see me." He walked back to his desk, leaving his office door open and my mouth ajar.

Kitt's aunt Eleanor was visiting Mr. C? *Whatever for*? Kitt had

mentioned nothing beyond the fact that her aunt Ellie didn't think too much of Mr. C, that she'd known the Caboodles way back when. Maybe she was just stopping by to say hello. But that didn't explain his obvious anxiety, though. It seemed worse than usual.

I was pondering the smallness of a world that linked Eleanor Kitt, formerly of Backhoe, Nebraska and Mr. Caboodle of the upper crust East-Coast Caboodles and investment banking fame, when the daytime glass doors swung open and Kitt's Aunt Ellie strode in. She was a tall woman, close to Kitt's height, with fading, reddish hair the color of old leaves that tend to hang onto their trees through the winter. She wore a purple suit and flat brown shoes. A swollen scarred-leather briefcase hung from her padded shoulder. She bore down on my desk, flashed the family's signature smile, and thrust out a large hand.

"You are Caroline," she said. "I am Kitt's Aunt Ellie."

"I could tell," I told her, returning her vigorous handshake. "Mr. C is waiting for you. Would you like some coffee?"

"Love some. Missy drinks that instant stuff. Disgusting."

"How do you like yours? Cream and sugar?"

"Black," she said, catching sight of Mr. C. "That way?" She gestured toward him with a jerk of her head.

"Go right in," I told her and left to get her coffee.

When I brought it in, the two were laughing over some distant shared memory and Eleanor Kitt was removing papers from her huge shoulder bag. She pushed them aside to make room for the coffee, saying, "Thanks, Caroline."

I closed the door behind me and saw nothing of either of them for the next four hours. This was indeed strange. Kitt was nowhere to be found, out on an important appointment that morning. The Royal Georges were both on business trips. Most of the other brokers were at a conference on technology stocks being held at a local hotel.

At 1 P.M., Harold, a Caboodle cousin, arrived and the three of them — Mr. C, Eleanor Kitt, and Cousin Harold — all went out to lunch. Why, Mr. C, I thought, you're keeping another secret from me. Something important is happening and I don't know what it is.

This sense was confirmed when Kitt arrived at about 2 o'clock. "Are they back?" she asked me.

"Any minute," I said. "They're out to lunch with Harold C."

"I know," she said, chewing her lip and looking distracted. So Kitt knew something. But I had no time to pump her because at that very moment, the two Mr. C's returned with Kitt's Aunt Ellie, all three looking jovial and well-fed.

"Okay, Missy Kitt," Mr. C said, "we need to have a long and serious talk together." Kitt followed the trio into Mr. C's office and once more the door was closed.

The only other person to enter that room during the afternoon was Chaddy Winkley, the head of Compliance, which is the legal department of Caboodle & Company. As befits his position, Mr. Winkley is serious to the point of being ponderous. "Chaddy" seems an unlikely name for him (his real name was Chaddiford). He just isn't the kind of guy to inspire nicknames. But he and Mr. C had grown up together on the social playgrounds of our town and so we all knew him by his childhood name of "Chaddy."

When Chaddy Winkley disappeared into the office in which Kitt sat with Mr. C, Harold C, and her very rich aunt Eleanor, I began to figure out what might be happening.

At about five o'clock, they emerged, talking excitedly, shaking hands, Mr. C ushering them out. All the faces were wreathed in smiles.

By that time, the desks were occupied by the other brokers who'd returned from the technology conference and were now looking over their messages. As Mr. C began to speak to the departing Chaddy, the brokers all looked up from their fistsful of pink slips.

"So we'll make the general announcement in the morning, Chaddy, is that right?"

"That's right. We're okay with the SEC and the NASD. Also, the stock exchanges. We'll get the name change in the *Journal*, the *Investors' Business Daily* and *The New York Times*."

Name change? Kitt, looking slightly stunned, shook Mr. Winkley's hand, who in turn shook the hand of Aunt Ellie, who stood serenely in the center of the group, holding a piece of paper. She handed it to me without comment.

"FOR IMMEDIATE RELEASE:
Caboodle & Company To Become Kitt & Caboodle

Last night Caboodle & Company announced a name change, a senior management change, and an addition to the senior management team. With the adding of Ms. Eleanor Kitt to its senior management, the 80-year-old firm has, effective immediately, changed its name to Kitt & Caboodle. In addition, Ms. Kitt and her niece, Ms. Missy Kitt, have both joined the firm's executive committee.

Ms. Eleanor Kitt, a professional investor from New York City, has participated in the resurgence of several major NYSE companies as both venture capitalist and board member. She will take an active part in the firm's management, but does not plan to relocate from her New York City office.

Ms. Missy Kitt has been employed as a broker by Caboodle & Company for nearly seven years, during which time she has taken an active role in both the firm's investment banking and research divisions. She was also instrumental in the IPO for Mom's Mums."

CHAPTER NINE: MANAGING PORTFOLIOS

Asking the Basic Questions

Over the next few years, changes occurred which, in themselves, were not drastic but, when taken together, signaled an important new direction for Kitt & Caboodle. The front room was redesigned. Wall-to-wall carpeting was put in place, as were new doors.

The carved oak monster-doors that felt like you were moving giant redwoods when you arrived in the morning now stood open permanently, and regular security doors, which slid easily on a track, were installed.

These things may not seem like much but, for me, they were emblematic of the ease with which new opportunities would open for K&C with Ms. Eleanor at the helm, Kitt at her side, and Mr. C stumbling along behind, trying to keep up.

During a period when K&C was witness to virtually every kind of economic "season" that politics and events could visit upon us, short of a return to the Dark Ages, The Four-Season Portfolio became the core concept of our money management business. Through it all, I've been happy to have my money on and in the Four-Season Portfolio.

One thing I've learned about Kitt after working with her all these years: She's much more comfortable if she can lay a formula on something. I mean, she likes to have a standard way to approach things. I told her of my theory about her, and she agreed, "Yup. You're right. At least I like to start with a set of steps or a formula. It keeps me from making impetuous decisions. It keeps me from falling for every stock story I hear. And it takes the emotion out of stock-picking and portfolio management."

"Emotion?" I repeated. "How does emotion figure in?"

"Well, maybe I mean panic and over-enthusiasm. Both of them can affect investment decisions," she said. "Thanks to the Caboodles, I've nailed down the five things I need to know about every single portfolio that I manage, including ours."

"Okay. What are they?" I pulled out our investment notebook and a pencil.

"Well, you really know them already. First, what's the purpose of the portfolio? Second, what is its time horizon? Third, how much money is available for investment? Fourth, how much risk is acceptable? And fifth, what are the tax considerations? Answering those questions helps me to organize a portfolio plan for just about anybody."

Mr. C and his Wealthy Chauffeur

Remember when I told you about Mr. C's elderly driver named Charles? Charles is more like Mr. C's great-uncle or grandfather than his chauffeur, especially now that he's so old that Mr. C does all the driving for the two of them. Not long ago, Mr. C told me the story of Charles's retirement plan.

When Charles was about 70, Mr. C realized he had no retirement money except for what Social Security might pay him. Mr. C felt awful. How could he let Charles retire without *any* pension? So he told Charles he would give him $10,000 a year for the next ten years. At the time, $10,000 seemed like a huge amount of money, and, with it, Mr. C expected Charles to retire somewhere and live the high life.

Charles, on the other hand, had no intention of retiring and was quite insulted when Mr. C suggested it. "I promised your father that I'd look after you, and I don't intend to do it from some beach somewhere, young man," was all he said.

Charles refused the $10,000 in retirement income and just kept showing up in his chauffeur suit and cap and sliding behind the wheel of whatever car Mr. C owned at the time. (This was a good thing, since Mr. C didn't really learn how to drive very well until Charles turned eighty.)

Mr. C, somewhat stealthily, stuck to his guns, though. Each year, he invested $10,000 in the same, good stock mutual fund, letting it reinvest

all the dividends and capital gains. This went on for ten years.

When Charles turned eighty, he began to slow down some and it looked like he finally might retire. So Mr. C told him that, despite Charles's comments at the time, he'd invested the retirement money for him. And he presented Charles with the latest statement from the mutual fund, which, lo and behold, showed him in the possession of $225,000! When Mr. C told me about this, I was astounded.

So Charles retired and for the *next* ten years, while also receiving Social Security, he drew out enough money from the mutual fund each year to support himself.

"He started withdrawing 10% of the value, Caroline. That was the first year. After that, he withdrew the 10% plus an amount equal to whatever the consumer price index had risen that year. The mutual fund company worked it all out for us."

"Has he run out of money yet?" I asked. After ten years, taking out at least ten percent a year, you'd think he'd have been pretty close to scraping the bottom. At least, I thought so.

"Hah!" cried Mr. C. "Not even close!" He fumbled in his suit's coat-pocket and pulled out a folded paper, laying it on my desk. I saw that it was the statement from Charles's mutual fund company. "Just look at the value," Mr. C ordered.

To my astonishment, I saw that the fund was now worth over $560,000! And this was after ten years of withdrawals and no more contributions by Mr. C.

I was so dazzled by this that I told Kitt to put some of our money into the same mutual fund. She agreed that it was a terrific idea, especially since we had much more than ten years before our retirement(s).

The Endowment Fund Portfolio

It was Mr. C's experience with Charles and his retirement money that Kitt was thinking about when she returned to the office one day after doing her volunteer work at a local nonprofit agency. This agency had originally been endowed by the Caboodle Foundation, and, over the years, Caboodle & Company employees would help out with time and

donations. Every couple of weeks, Kitt would spend a lunch hour counseling unemployed people on personal budgeting problems. She always enjoyed this, but on one particular day, she seemed especially pleased.

"You'll never guess what happened," she said to me.

"You're right," I replied. "So just tell me."

"One of our former unemployeds died last week."

"How awful. But it *does* happen — all the time."

"Seems that one of the items she always took care of, through thick and thin, was her insurance premium."

"So?"

"Well, she outlived her primary beneficiary and the policy proceeds are now coming to the secondary beneficiary — us. The Agency. Or, rather, to the Agency Endowment Fund."

"No!" I said, amazed.

"Yes, and now we have to figure out what to do with it. As the Agency's financial counselor, the job has fallen to me."

"And a good thing it has. What are you going to do?"

"Gotta think about it." She went to her desk and proceeded to ponder.

The Endowment from the early Caboodles helped support a small, paid staff and little more. The Agency also had to rely on a few small grants and donations of money and time by volunteers like Kitt. These volunteers often used their own office resources to do a lot of the necessary administrative work. This was not a good policy for the long haul, but with such a small endowment, it was one the Agency was stuck with.

Then, along came the inheritance and Kitt's plan. It was a simple one, based, of course, on the Four-Season Portfolio and on Charles' Retirement Plan.

"First, you've got to find out what the purpose of the portfolio is," Kitt said, both to me and to herself. "Remember the portfolio questions?

"What is its time horizon? After that, I need to know how much money is available for investment and how much risk is acceptable. Last thing to ask: What are the tax considerations?"

"Okay." I waited for the answers.

"The purpose is to support the Agency so that it can continue to offer counseling services to unemployed people. That means, it has to

pay for the office staff — which is really just Mrs. Kenilworth. She runs the whole operation with her computer. But she wants to hire an assistant. And she needs to upgrade the office copier, and buy a fax machine, stuff like that.

"So the Endowment needs to yield enough income to supplement the grants and donations that the Agency gets now, in order to cover the annual budget. Right now, it's entirely invested in bonds. Sure, they pay income, but the Endowment's purchasing power has dwindled so much that it really doesn't help much."

"Sounds sort of like the McWeedies, doesn't it?" I said.

"Right. The problem isn't dissimilar to that of most retirees. They need income now, but also need enough growth to be sure their money holds out their whole lives."

"So the answer to the second question — the time horizon one — is the whole life of the Agency?"

"Yes. And that's forever. At least, Mrs. Kenilworth and all the counselees hope it is. So, given that LONG time horizon, you need to have some of the money in something that grows and continues to grow.

"Okay." I wrote that down and then asked the next question on her list, "How much money is available for investment?"

"The inheritance is $300,000. Add that to the Caboodle money and you come up with $400,000. And to answer the next question, very little risk can be taken with this money.

"But one thing we know, Caroline: The risk you take with fixed income is also real. You may not lose the dollar amount by putting it all in treasuries, but the dollar itself loses value. That's what's happening now because of inflation. So we have to consider that to be a risk."

"Okay. Last question: Tax considerations. Are endowment funds taxable?"

"No. So we don't have to worry about paying tax on the income."

Kitt's plan, which she presented to the Agency Board of Directors, consisted of adding $100,000 to the Autumn and Winter seasons of the Agency Endowment Fund by buying $50,000 of treasuries that matured every five years, and putting $50,000 into a top-quality utility fund. These things were yielding between 5% to 7% at the time, but the dividends on the utilities were going up each year.

The utility fund was one of Kitt's favorites. It had a five-star Morningstar rating, and a manager with long and successful experience who included high quality REITs, as well as telephone utilities, in his fund. He even had some foreign phone companies in there at the time Kitt bought the fund for the Agency. So a little bit of Autumn was sort of late Summer. The fund's annual expense ratio (annual expenses, excluding brokerage costs, as a percentage of total fund assets) was only 1.2%.

"This fund has increased its dividend every year. The fund's value has gone up substantially, too," she said to me, somewhat unnecessarily, since we held it in our joint portfolio, too.

"What are you going to do for Spring and Summer?" I asked.

"Ah. That's the interesting part. I'm buying them an excellent growth stock mutual fund and we'll reinvest all capital gains. But by putting them on a withdrawal plan that takes 6% out every year, they can use it to supplement the income from Autumn and Winter. The withdrawals should take care of the costs of inflation."

I was confused. "How can you take that much out and still have money left to grow for the Spring and Summer seasons?" But my question sounded familiar to me. I had asked the same thing about Charles's retirement money. I answered it myself.

"I'll bet you expect to have more left in ten years than you start with today."

"That's what I expect. I sent for a company illustration of what would have happened if we did this from 1985 to 1995. Look at this." She pulled out a sheet of paper with the mutual fund company's logo on top and laid it on my desk.

"This fund is one of the oldest in the country, has an excellent Morningstar rating, an experienced manager, and a low risk profile. It invests in mostly adult companies with a few teens. "It *IS* a load fund. But its history of performing better than its benchmark during down markets is excellent. I like this fund for the Agency Endowment because I have so much confidence in the manager."

"Too bad you have to pay a front-end load for it," I commented.

"True. But because we'll be buying $200,000 worth, we get a quantity discount. The commission goes down to 3.5%, so the amount that actually gets invested is $193,000. Remember, you have to deduct the

load first. Then the remainder goes into the mutual fund.

"But the annual expense ratio for this fund is extremely low, only about 6/10 of one percent. That's about half of what the average fund charges for expenses annually. So it's cheaper in the long run than some no-load funds with higher annual costs."

The Board of Directors loved Kitt's plan, especially her decision to take her commission from the front-end loaded growth mutual fund, and make it her annual donation to the Agency.

With the yield from its Autumn and Winter investments, and the annual withdrawals from the growth mutual fund, the income from the Endowment Fund's Four Season Portfolio should be around 6% of the total $400,000 invested, or $24,000 a year. This will be sufficient to cover Mrs. Kenilworth's modest salary and to have some operating expense money left over to boot.

And, if all goes according to plan, the value of the growth mutual fund will go up over the years. The committee will be taking 6% out of an increasing amount of money, allowing the Agency to cover costs inevitably higher due to inflation.

The Family Inheritance Portfolio

The Grandpa Portfolio gave Kitt the biggest headache during her initial year with the Four-Season Plan.

"This is a clear case of Too Many Cooks Spoiling the Broth, Caroline," she told me one day, after an extended phone call with her folks failed to produce any agreement on how to allocate the investment money.

"What does Miss Eleanor think about it?" I asked. I knew that Kitt and her aunt spoke to each other on the phone almost every day, even though Miss E lived in New York and appeared at K&C's offices only rarely.

"She's left the whole thing in my hands. Says to do what I think is best."

"So, what do you think is best?"

"The problem is deciding for whom we're investing this money.

I mean, if the allocations are based on age, whose age do we use? Mom and Dad want to hang up their hoes pretty soon and turn the farm over to the Backhoe Kitts."

"So use your folks' ages. What's the problem with that?"

"They tell me they want growth, even aggressive growth. They say they don't need the income and don't like the Autumn and Winter part of my plan. They want to build a big inheritance for all of us — the Kitt cousins and progeny."

"Hmmmm. What are you going to do?"

"I need to convince them that there won't be any way to replace big losses if investments in aggressive growth stocks go sour. Then nobody would get anything." Her face lit up as only her face can.

"That's it. The key to allocation between the different kinds of growth stocks is understanding a portfolio's replacement potential. If a person is young enough to make up losses with her own income, then aggressive growth makes some sense.

"But if the original pot of gold is all there's ever going to be, it's much smarter to stick with the adult companies whose earnings are predictable and from whom there are few surprises."

"Dull, but probably true," I agreed.

"And I need to ask my usual five questions: What's the purpose of the portfolio, what's its time horizon, how much money is available, how much risk is acceptable, and what are the tax considerations?"

Kitt passed this on to her parents and, to her surprise, they understood. Here's the plan she put together for the Grandpa Portfolio. Its aim — and eventual result — was slow but steady growth and some income, too.

One feature of the plan that pleased Kitt's folks was that the income would be invested in what Kitt called the Progeny's mutual funds: A separate account that held mutual funds to be used for the education of next-generation Kitts. The account was in the form of a trust, for the benefit of the named grandchildren.

Kitt chose mutual funds that accepted additional contributions as small as $50 and instructed the back office of K&C to "sweep" any income from the Grandpa Portfolio into these mutual funds as soon as it was paid.

"I'm using an aggressive growth stock fund for the Progeny accounts. That makes the folks happy. Since it won't be the ONLY source of college money, it's worth the risk.

"AND it can be replaced by the income from the Grandpa Portfolio, so it answers the replacement potential question with a yes."

The College Education Portfolio

One of Kitt's other accounts was with a young lawyer named Mitch and his wife Susan. They were in their thirties and doing fairly well at their jobs. But the expense of a new home and baby took most of their income, and they found themselves at night worrying about how to get baby Joey through college.

"We're putting as much as we're allowed into our 401K plans, but that's really for *our* retirement. How can we set money aside for our children's education — Joey's and whoever comes next?" they asked Kitt.

Since Susan and Mitch had no personal investment portfolio outside their 401K plans, there was no way to use the Grandpa Portfolio strategy: reinvesting income from a master portfolio into an auxiliary Progeny account.

"Buy a mutual fund in Joey's name with you as custodian," Kitt counseled, "preferably one that has a low initial investment requirement. Then arrange to have the mutual fund company deduct the minimum additional investment (as low as $50) from your checking account every month.

"This may require sacrifice on your part, but probably not much. These days, $50 represents a dinner out with a movie. If you factor in the babysitter, you'll probably be investing less each month on Joey's account than you'd pay for one evening's entertainment. In the name of Joey's education, stay home that night and rent a video. And, of course, anybody can make contributions to this account — especially grandparents."

Mitch and Susan liked the idea and set up the account.

"How about zero-coupon bonds for Joey?" I asked, when Kitt relayed this conversation to me. "Wouldn't they be good investments for college, too?"

"Yes. It was my suggestion that, as the mutual fund grows into a substantial investment, and if interest rates are high enough to make zeros attractive, they should liquidate some shares of the fund and buy zero coupon treasuries that mature in the years that Joey is 18 through 20.

"Until he turns fourteen, the parents will have to pay tax, based on their tax bracket, on any income over $500 a year that comes from the treasury zeros, but at least treasuries can't be called away, the way municipal or corporate bonds can be."

"Called away," as Kitt explained it to me, means that the issuer of municipal and corporate bonds can pay the bonds off earlier than the original maturity date. They do this if interest rates go a lot lower than they were when the bonds were issued. If that happens, they can refinance the bonds at a lower interest cost. So, whoosh, bonds you counted on for income during Winters are gone from the portfolio and itty-bitty-yielding cash is put in their place.

"Most bonds," added Kitt, "have call protection for buyers, meaning that the bonds can't be called before a certain date. But if interest rates go down a lot, you can bet that your high-yielding bonds are going to be called as soon as that time is up. At that point, it's goodbye high yield."

Then Kitt told me about something that happened to the McWeedies. They'd bought some zero-coupon municipal bonds back when interest rates were so high that they had to pay only about $350 for $1000 of face value when the bonds matured. In all, they paid around $17,000 and planned to get $50,000 a few years into their retirement.

"That bond issue had serial maturities of zeros," Kitt said.

"Come again?" I asked.

"There were zero coupon bonds coming due in consecutive years, the years when the McWeedies would be in their late sixties and early seventies. So they bought fifty of each, and thought they were set to collect a nice amount when they matured, one right after the other."

"So what happened?"

"Well, the bonds had ten-year call protection. They couldn't be called for ten years. The ten years were up last December and sure enough, the bonds got called. All of them. So now the McWeedies have the money back that they paid for the bonds, but interest rates are so much lower now that the money they got back won't buy nearly as much in the way

of face value.

"If they had bought zero-coupon treasury bonds, they couldn't have been called. But they hadn't wanted to pay tax on the income each year, because they weren't actually collecting it. They were terribly disappointed when their nice retirement supplement was called away.

"They should have bought the zero coupon treasuries and put them in their IRAs."

"Huh?" I said.

"Remember, the IRA name refers to the account that someone has for his or her retirement: the Individual Retirement Account. By today's law, you can put up to $2,000 into it each year and not pay taxes on that money (unless you, or another person in the family, has some other pension account). If you do, you can still put money into the IRA, and it can still grow without being taxed, but the initial contribution to the IRA has to be with after-tax dollars.

"Lots of people think that an IRA is a Certificate of Deposit in a bank account and that you can have only one. That's incorrect."

"It is?" I asked, thinking of my puny little IRA, vegging out at the local bank in a 3% CD.

"It is. You can have as many as you want, as long as you don't put in more than the allowed amount each year. And you can fund the Individual Retirement Account with stocks and bonds, as well as mutual funds and certificates of deposit."

"So the McWeedies could've put the money they used for the zero coupon municipals into non-callable treasury zeros and stashed them into an IRA?"

"That's right."

This is a good thing to remember: There are different kinds of zero-coupon bonds. One variety is issued by the Treasury. Another is offered by corporations and municipalities. The big question to ask about any of them is: Can they be called away from you? How are they taxed? Can they be sheltered from taxes in an IRA or some other kind of IRS-qualified retirement account?

I now turned my attention, and our discussion, back to Joey and the rising cost of going to college. "How do you figure out how much money they'll need for tuition?"

"Oh, we can plug inflation rates of 2-5% a year into today's tuition costs, but the truth is that I have no idea. Tuition rates have gone up much faster than inflation. Who really knows what college is going to cost in the future? I tell people that they can only make their best guess and hope that it's good enough."

STARTING FROM SCRATCH

That was the situation with Mitch, Susan, and Joey. One day, Susan's sisters, Betsy and Sally, came in to talk with Kitt about *their* investing. They had each saved a few thousand dollars and wanted to get started but didn't know how. Later, Kitt came over to my desk and told me about their meeting.

"They're both in their early twenties, a great time to get started. They both have good jobs and no huge expenses yet. Neither one is married.

"I told them about the Four Season Portfolio Plan and they liked it. We decided that they should allocate about 80% to the Spring and Summer seasons and no more than 20% to Autumn and Winter."

"How do you manage that with only a few thousand dollars?"

"Not easy. Mutual funds are really the best kind of investment if you, like Betsy and Sally, don't have a lot of money to begin with. And lots of mutual funds require that you have a minimum of a couple of thousand dollars to begin with.

"I asked if they could get into their company's 401-K plans. Mutual fund companies don't usually impose any minimum for 401-K investments and lots of times, mutual funds lower their minimum investment requirements for IRAs, too. It turns out that neither one could get into a company 401-K, but Sally eventually will be eligible for her company's profit-sharing plan.

"So I suggested IRAs because neither one of them is covered by any other kind of pension plan at their place of employment. Even when Sally is finally eligible for the company's profit sharing plan, she could still contribute to her IRA and deduct the contribution if the company HAS no profits and therefore doesn't share anything.

"And she can always have an IRA and fund it with after-tax dollars.

So can Betsy. The investments grow tax-free. They don't have to pay tax on any income or capital gains." Kitt placed a pile of account forms on my desk and handed me some checks.

"I'm opening regular investment accounts for them, too. That way they can invest more than the $2000 a year maximum they're allowed in the IRAs."

"But these aren't enough for Four-Season Portfolios," I remarked, noting the amount written on the checks: $4200 from Betsy and $4350 from Sally.

"Not if we buy them individual stocks. I'd have to buy odd lots" (fewer than the hundred shares which are considered a "round lot") " … and I hate to do that," she murmured as she wrote.

"You end up with little bits of companies, and, after paying all those commissions, you have to have humongous moves in the stock prices to make any real money. Oh, damn," she said. "I just wrote 'Humongous' instead of the name of the fund I'm buying for Betsy."

"So you're buying mutual funds instead and putting them into the IRAs," I concluded, picking up the ticket for The Humongous Fund. "Great name."

Kitt laughed and took the ticket out of my hand, ripping it in half. She picked up a blank ticket from the stack on my desk and started to fill it out.

"I'm buying four funds for each of them. A growth stock fund, an international fund, a utility fund (this one has equity REITs in it, too) and a bond fund. But notice, please, that I have spent only about 20% of the total on the bond and utility funds combined. The other 80% is in the growth stock fund and the international fund. At their ages, they should have most of their money in growth."

"How in heaven's name do you know which funds to buy?" I asked. "There are about a zillion mutual funds to choose from these days."

"The same way I choose stocks. I have certain criteria — you know, those reasons we want to own something. I look for those criteria in the funds ranked four- and five-star by Morningstar. I want to know who the manager is and how long he or she has been managing, how well he or she has done relative to the benchmark that fund is using …"

"Hold on!" I said. "What do you mean by benchmark?"

"Well, you have to have some way of measuring the value added by the professional managers. You are, after all, paying for their expertise. Remember that management fee?" Kitt reached over my desk to the display of mutual fund prospectuses against the wall.

"Load-fund or no-load fund, of the money you've invested, you still pay anywhere from a half to three percent for management and other expenses." She flipped through the pages and found what she was looking for. "Here," she added, pointing to a paragraph entitled "Fees and Other Expenses." "This is what you have to pay for these people to make decisions on what to buy and sell in your fund."

Closing the little brochure, she continued, "If you pay the management fee, you'll certainly want to know if they're worth the additional cost. If they aren't, you might as well put the money into an index fund."

"Explain, please." I knew I should know this stuff, having worked at Caboodle & Company as long as I had, but I didn't.

"Index funds just buy and hold stocks that mirror the major indexes, like the Standard & Poor's 500. They don't manage at all.

"The indexes — Standard & Poor's 500 Index (that's made up of 500 of the largest public companies in the U.S.), Standard & Poor's Midcap Index (this one is 400 companies that are smaller than those in the S&P 500), and the Russell 2000 Index (2000 of the more aggressive, smaller companies) are called benchmarks because whatever happens to the indexes during a time period — if their value goes up or down — it happens *without* any management added. So funds with management added should really do better than the *un*managed index.

"You use as a benchmark the index which has the same kind of stocks as are in the mutual fund you own. Then you can see how well the mutual fund manager has done relative to the unmanaged index."

"So how would anyone find that out? Is it in the prospectus?"

"Yes. Morningstar and *Value Line* Mutual Fund Rankings also report on the manager's performance relative to the fund's benchmark. And in more detail. It's really best to check either one of those for the most complete information."

"The S&P 500 is the benchmark for the mutual funds of large, adult-type companies. But I'm buying a more aggressive fund for Betsy and Sally: It has teenagers and some baby companies in it. I think the Russell

2000 is a better index for that fund, but I'll see what Morningstar uses.

"For the other three funds, the EAFE (that's the Europe Australia Far East Index) is an okay benchmark for the international fund. It doesn't say anything in its title about the Western Hemisphere, so I guess there aren't any companies from North, Central, or South America in it. It's definitely not the perfect international benchmark, but it's okay for now.

"For utilities, the benchmark is Standard & Poor's Utility Index. Duff and Phelps also has a utility index.

"And the Lehman Brothers Bond Index is one that can be used as a benchmark for the Winter investments.

"Now, Caroline, I don't want to confuse you, but you should know before you get a day older that there are two different kinds of mutual funds," Kitt said.

"I know *that*," I scoffed. I did. Really.

More About Mutual Funds: Open- and Closed-End

Here, I'll prove it. There are closed-end and open-ended mutual funds. The closed-end funds raise money just like Mom's Mums did, in an initial public offering, and then use that money to buy the stocks of companies. The closed-end funds are more like regular companies whose business it is to invest in other companies. And after a closed-end fund invests the money it's raised, it trades on a stock exchange, just like regular stock.

The open-ended mutual funds are different because they aren't "closed" to new customers, but offer new shares all the time. Also, the mutual fund company redeems or buys back shares whenever somebody decides they want to sell. Some have "loads" or commissions attached that don't have anything to do with the fund's regular expenses, but are used to pay the broker who sells them.

In fact, a "front-end" load is taken right off the top before the rest of the money is put into the fund. So if you have $10,000 to invest in a mutual fund with a 5% front-end load, the 5% or $500 is deducted right away for the broker and the remaining $9500 is put into the fund.

Some mutual fund companies offer alternative ways to pay the broker. Shares with upfront sales charges are classified as "A" shares. If they're called "B," "C," or something similar, the broker gets paid in one of two ways: when you sell your mutual fund shares or during the time you hold them through a "12-B-1" charge. You can find out this important detail by reading the section on fees and sales charges in the prospectus. Make a point of doing this if you've been told that the fund sold to you by a broker is "no-load."

Others are sold without loads ("no-load"), but these may have higher operating expenses, including special distribution fees called "12B-1 charges." All the fees are listed in the prospectus.

At the end of each business day, some computer in the mutual fund company figures out how much the assets behind each share are worth. It takes the value of each company's stock the fund has invested in and divides it up among all the shares they've sold. This is called the "net asset value," or "NAV," of the shares.

Net asset value goes up and down as the value in the stocks the mutual fund holds goes up and down. You can find the net asset value of your mutual fund shares by looking it up in the newspaper. It's under the column headed "NAV."

If a mutual fund charges a load, it'll be added on and listed under the "offered" column.

Closed-end funds, on the other hand, sell at whatever price the public is willing to pay for them, just like all the other listed stocks. Closed-end funds can sell at a discount to their net asset value. Sometimes, they sell at a higher price than their NAV, at a "premium" in other words.

I asked Kitt, "So what are some other criteria for deciding on a mutual fund?"

"Naturally, I want to make sure that the fund has had better than average performance over the past several years, but it doesn't have to be the top-performer. A fund could be #1 because one or two of its stocks got bought out or because it just happened to have chosen the right industry to invest in. It's hard to pull that off year after year."

She thought for a minute and then added, "I prefer to buy a fund that's been around for at least three years. And I *never* buy a closed-end fund at a premium to its net asset value or on the initial public offering."

Most of the international funds that invest in a single country or region are closed-end mutual funds. So are the bulk of the utility funds and the REIT funds.

"Is that all?" I was writing down these criteria for future reference.

"No. One last thing: I look at Morningstar's report to see how well the fund's manager has done relative to other people who manage the same kind of mutual fund. It helps to answer the question, why buy THIS fund instead of THAT fund? And, of course, I write down the reasons I have bought THIS fund so that I can keep track of its progress, just as we do with regular stocks."

In my investment notebook, I listed the following criteria by which to judge a mutual fund:

MUTUAL FUND CHECKLIST

1. Who is the manager?
2. How long has he/she been managing the fund?
3. What has been the fund's performance relative to the appropriate benchmark?
4. How well has this manager done compared to other managers of this kind of fund?
5. What does it cost to invest in this fund: load, 12-B-1 charge, management fees?

CHAPTER 10: KEEPING UP

Kitt and The Perfectly Passive Investor

"I hate stocks. I hate bonds. I've never made money in any of 'em." The man who sat at Kitt's desk told her this in a voice that dared disagreement. His name was Jackson, he had told me when he charged up to my desk. Someone had suggested that he talk to Kitt.

Mr. Jackson was a long, thin, nervous person whose legs alternately stretched out in front of him or bent at the knees and bounced up and down as he talked. He simply couldn't keep his appendages still. His fingers tapped, his arms waved, his feet crossed and uncrossed, and his legs kept folding and unfolding. The man was a fidgety wreck.

Kitt spoke soothingly. "You've had a bad experience with the market, I guess. What happened?"

"How the hell should I know what happened?" His voice rose. "I follow the advice of somebody like you who's supposed to know what's going on and I lose money every time." He went on to name some of his investments that had gone sour.

"Those were pretty aggressive investments, Mr. Jackson," Kitt began. "Was that what you wanted?" Wrong question. The man's face turned the shade of clay.

"Lady, what I wanted was to make money. I told the guy, 'You're the expert. Make me money.' He said, 'Okay.' So he puts me into this and that and every single thing went south."

I waited for Kitt to tell him that he should've done his homework, that he should've had *some* idea of the risks he was taking, just as she always told that to me. I was wondering if I should dive under my desk or call 911 when she responded, "No wonder you're upset. You have every right to be angry."

Huh? Of course, she had to soothe the guy, but I thought she was laying it on a little thick. Telling an inquiring broker that your "investment objectives are to make money" is like telling an architect you want a roof over your head. It borders on what my mother would call "smart-alecky."

Kitt was saying, "It's hard to know what questions to ask a broker, isn't it?" The man stopped his tapping and folding and looked at Kitt.

"There are all sorts of ways to 'make money' in the market, Mr. Jackson. And to lose it, too. A customer really needs to be told what risks there are to each kind of investment. And the broker needs to know your time horizon."

"What the hell does that mean?" said Mr. Jackson, who was firing up again.

"How long are you willing to hold your stocks, how much time can you keep your money invested?"

"This is supposed to be my retirement money." He looked about forty. "I told him to make me rich." This was followed by a snort. "I knew that people made a lot of money in the stock market. You hear about it all the time."

"It's certainly possible. But gardens don't grow by throwing seed out your back door and hoping for the best." Mr. Jackson looked puzzled.

"Let me tell you about the Four-Season Portfolio Plan," Kitt continued, reaching into her desk for the illustration she always used with new customers.

"No, thanks. If that plan has anything to do with stocks, count me out," said Mr. Jackson, his knees resuming their bouncing.

Kitt sighed and closed her desk drawer. "What *is it* that I can do for you, Mr. Jackson?"

"I don't know. My wife heard you talk somewhere. Said you sounded like you knew what you were talking about." He was calmer now. "I know I have to do something, but I can't stand the idea of dealing with another broker." He looked at Kitt suspiciously and asked, "Is that what you are?"

"Yes," she said. "And I don't think you should deal with another broker either." Kitt opened another drawer and pulled out a brochure, handing it to him.

"I think what you should consider are index funds. They seem to me

to be perfect for the passive investor."

This guy was passive? Passive/Aggressive, maybe. Anyway, while he was looking at the brochure, Kitt continued, "See, a customer really needs to know how active a money manager he wants to be. It is *your* responsibility to make the investment decisions, not the broker's. You have to know something about the stocks you're investing in." Mr. Jackson looked up from his reading. I thought he might change color again, but this time he said nothing.

And Kitt moved forward. "If you don't want to have anything to do with investment decisions, and you don't want anyone else making those decisions to buy and sell stocks for you, the best thing for you is an index fund. Better yet, a couple of index funds."

She went on to explain that index funds were mutual funds that invested in the same companies that were in specific market indexes, like the Standard & Poor's 500. The Standard & Poor's is made up of 500 of the country's largest companies, so an index fund that exactly replicates it holds the same 500 stocks. Other Standard & Poor's Index Funds might not reproduce all 500, but a substantial number of representative stocks.

"There are indexes for over a hundred specific markets now and index mutual funds you can buy that'll give you the same market performance as each of those indexes."

She told Mr. Jackson that he could choose a couple of indexes that have done well over the years, buy the index funds that held those stocks, and hold onto them until he retired. No need to read quarterly or annual reports, no need to understand much of anything. He could be a totally passive investor, because the index fund won't change any of its holdings unless the index itself does. And that happens only rarely.

"But you need to pick the index funds that replicate the indexes *completely* or, at least, track the benchmark index very closely. Some indexes are so huge — like the Wilshire 5000, which actually follows almost 7000 companies — that the index fund would have to be a sample of those stocks."

"Can somebody make money in something like that? An index fund?" Mr. Jackson asked.

"Now, Mr. Jackson," Kitt admonished, "I suspect you want to get rich quick. You've got to get rid of that notion. People don't get rich quick in

the stock market unless the circumstances are very unusual. What's wrong with getting rich slow?"

"You used an adjective to modify a verb," Mr. Jackson said.

"I beg your pardon?"

"You asked, 'What was wrong with getting rich slow?' I said you used an adjective to modify a verb. It should be 'getting rich slow*ly*.'" He paused, calmer now. "I used to be an English teacher." Kitt laughed.

"Okay then. Let's get you rich slow*ly*. And let me explain to you exactly how this is supposed to happen. And how some years things will be good and some years things will be bad. And how you have to leave the money alone to *let* it grow. Okay?"

She went on to explain both the advantages and the disadvantages of index fund investing. Besides getting very close to the same performance as the index and not having to rely on a portfolio manager making the right decisions, another advantage is that the expenses of an index fund are very low. Naturally, this makes sense because there's no real "management" involved. Some of these funds have expense ratios of less than two-tenths of one percent. Actively managed mutual funds, I remembered, often have expense ratios of 1 1/2 to 2% (which is deducted every year).

Index funds have a low portfolio turnover rate, too. They sell a stock only if it leaves the benchmark or because there are a lot of redemptions. That can happen if the market is really lousy and people want to get out. But most index funds keep about 10% of their money in cash to take care of large redemptions. So instead of a 50% or a 100% or even a 150% portfolio turnover, such as you might get in an actively managed stock fund, the turnover in an index fund is usually 10% or less.

Another big advantage to low portfolio turnover: When a manager isn't doing a lot of buying and selling, the costs are lower. And the capital gains tax you have to pay is lower, too. Because the stocks in the index fund aren't being sold for capital gain.

One of the difficulties, Kitt explained, is to make sure that the index funds really do mirror the index you choose. If the expense ratio is high, or if the performance is significantly different than the index itself (it will be slightly different because of the cash the fund holds which, of course, isn't moving with the index), it isn't really doing what you want it to do.

"You can find out from Morningstar what you need to know about index funds," Kitt told Mr. Jackson. "Morningstar tracks over 100 index funds and tells you all about expense ratios and past performance."

"Well, which ones should I buy? Or should I buy just one?" he asked.

"If I were you, I'd buy index funds that track the Russell 2000, the S&P Midcap, and the S&P 500 indexes. Then you'll have covered small, medium, and large companies. Then I'd add one index fund that tracks international stocks, like the Europe, Australia, Far East Index (EAFE) and a bond index fund, too.

"Strangely, the bond index funds have higher turnovers and expenses because the indexes change the bonds on them more often than, say, the Standard & Poor's, which almost never changes its holdings.

"If you decide to do this, you'll have five index funds that would cover just about every kind of investment and you'd be able to forget about making any buy and sell decisions at the wrong time.

"Just don't be tempted to try to outperform the indexes by trading indexes.

"Mr. Jackson," Kitt concluded, "I think this may be the answer for you. This is a strategy for the truly totally passive investor. To do well with it, you need to give it time. And leave it alone."

With all his bouncing around and angry tones, Mr. Jackson didn't strike me as a truly totally passive anything, but he seemed interested and asked if she could open an account and buy the index funds for him.

"You don't need me to do this for you. There are some wonderful no-load index funds that you can buy directly from the fund.

"Now, if you want to use the index funds as a core to your overall investment plan, and own other securities that would be more actively managed, I can handle it for an annual fee. Or I could buy (I don't often sell) stocks and bonds for you. I'd charge you only for the commissions.

"But I don't think you want that. And if you did, I'd make you promise to learn everything about any investments before we made them. I'd make you do your homework and prohibit you from ever, EVER saying you 'just want to make money.'" She flashed her winning smile.

"It's up to you. Get back to me when you've made your decision, okay?" Kitt stood and so did Mr. Jackson. He shook her hand and mum-

bled something that sounded like "Thanks for your time" and left.

Not five minutes later, he reappeared. "I want to ask you one question, okay?" he began.

"Go ahead," Kitt said.

"This guy, this other broker ..." He hesitated, studying the floor as if trying to locate the words he wanted in the thick tufts of carpet. Kitt waited.

"... can I *sue him*?" Mr. Jackson looked up at Kitt. He sat down in the seat next to her desk, watching her face with expectation.

Kitt answered, "In the securities business, most disputes go to arbitration instead of to a regular court of law, Mr. Jackson. It's possible that you might want to take this one to arbitration.

"But tell me first, what did he do wrong?" Kitt opened her notebook, grabbed a pen, and wrote Mr. Jackson's name at the top of the page.

"Whaddya mean, what did he do wrong? He lost a lot of my money, that's what he did wrong." Mr. Jackson's face was taking on just a hint of coral. Uh-oh, I thought.

"You asked him to 'make you a lot of money,' isn't that right?" Kitt asked.

"Yeah. And he didn't do it."

"The stocks he bought for you were volatile — their prices go up and down a lot. They might very well have made you a lot of money given time and a good strong stock market."

"So what are you saying? I should have stayed with the guy?"

"No. I don't think buying individual stocks is for you. And I don't know this broker you dealt with." Kitt put her pen down and rolled her desk chair around to face Mr. Jackson directly.

"There are some unethical people in this business who buy and sell securities without the customer's permission. Or they buy securities that are unlike what the customer has wanted to buy — like aggressive growth stocks when the customer didn't want to take on that kind of risk.

"When that happens, I strongly suggest that you report it to the broker's branch office manager. If you aren't satisfied with the manager's response, then I'd consider arbitration. That kind of broker makes the rest of us look bad and should be booted out of the business." She rolled her chair back to her desk.

"But that's not what happened here. What happened here is that you gave a directive to a guy who tried to do what you wanted and it didn't work. At least, that's the way it looks to me. Both of you were at fault, not just him."

Mr. Jackson looked deflated, but not coral, which relieved me. Kitt continued, "People who buy stocks need to realize that they've taken on a personal responsibility. The stockbroker is just that — a *broker* of stocks. She or he can make suggestions to the customer, but it's your job to decide whether the suggestions are right for you."

"But you people are supposed to be the professionals!" Mr. Jackson retorted, though without his former fire.

"We're registered to buy and sell stocks. Trained in securities law, so we know not to manipulate the market or do something inappropriate for the customer ..."

"Losing my money was inappropriate." Jackson didn't give up the fight easily.

"But you implied to him that you were willing to take on risk. 'Make me money,' you said, without asking about the risks involved. Now, if it had been me, I wouldn't have allowed you to get away with that 'make me money' line. No one can guarantee that, in the short-term, stocks will make you money. With aggressive stocks, you've got to have patience and a tolerance for ups and downs.

"The broker should have prepared you for that, I agree. But I'm not sure you would have listened. Am I right?"

To his credit, Mr. Jackson considered this comment and question carefully, and then nodded agreement. "I guess you are. I thought you just bought something and it went up. I didn't really have the time to listen to a big lecture."

Kitt laughed. "Oh, the lecture isn't so big. It's sort of like reading the instructions on a chain saw before trying to cut down a tree. Know what I mean?" She stood and Mr. Jackson stood. He put out his hand and shook hers vigorously.

"Thanks," he said and left once again.

Mutual Fund Mania: Too much of a good thing

We both assumed that Kitt had heard the last of Mr. Jackson. But late one afternoon, Kitt and I were surprised to look up and see a very round young woman coming through the front doors. Most of the other brokers had already switched off their Quotrons and headed for home, so this late arrival made her way slowly but directly toward us.

She was pretty but pumped up, sort of like one of those Thanksgiving Day Parade balloons. In fact, I half expected her to start floating and bobbing up to the ceiling. "Is Missy Kitt in, please?" she asked in a soft Southern accent. "Ah don't have an appointment," she said apologetically, drawing out the words.

"No problem," I answered and nodded toward Kitt, who stood and smiled.

"I'm Kitt," she said to the woman.

"Oh, ah'm so gla-yud to meet you? Ah'm Ginna Jackson? Y'all were sooo nahce to mah hoosband?" I looked at Kitt and knew she was wondering if these were questions she was supposed to answer or just part of the Southern drawl. She decided on the latter and simply responded, "Oh, yes … Mr. Jackson. Well, I was happy to help. He said you had come to one of my seminars."

"Ah shoo-uh did. May ah sit down?"

"Please do." Kitt sat, too. "What can I do for you, Mrs. Jackson?"

"Oh, please, cawl me Ginna? Well, ah need your help," and she went on to explain her problem.

Mrs. Jackson was a collector of mutual funds. In contrast to her husband, she'd been cheerfully buying every new fund she'd heard or read about and now owned over a hundred.

"A hundred mutual funds?" Kitt asked in astonishment.

"Yes, ma'am." Mrs. Jackson hung her head. "Ah shoo-uh do."

Poor Mrs. Jackson. Er, Ginna. She was awash in mutual fund reports and statements and had no idea how much money she'd made, if any. She overindulged in mutual funds like some people do in alcohol.

"Talk about diversification on a grand scale," I commented to Kitt later, after Mrs. Jackson had departed with Kitt's Mutual Fund Mania

remedy: Scaling back to manageable size. Kitt handed me the new account form and said, "Not really. She had forty-eight growth funds alone — all with the S&P as a benchmark. Most of those funds own the same stocks. That's not going to lower risk if the S&P breaks down. All twenty-eight will go down at once.

"And think of all the management fees she's paying. She'd do better with one index fund, pay far less in fees, and probably get better performance."

"Did she like that idea?" I asked.

"No. Said it would take all the fun out of it."

"Probably true," I said. "And I can't imagine somebody like Mrs. Jackson being totally passive and just letting the index fund do its thing."

"Too cold-turkey," Kitt agreed. "I recommended that she cut back to one fund per strategy: Adult and teen companies, baby companies, an international fund, and a bond fund."

"Same as Mr. Jackson's index funds," I said.

"Right. I pointed that out. She was pleased that she might be able to outperform his indexes."

"So, is she going to sell all those funds?"

"Every last one of them." Kitt held up a fistful of sell orders. "Since she's reinvested all her dividends and capital gains and those are held at each company, we'll have to write each company to redeem them."

I knew well the wording on those letters: "Please liquidate all full and fractional shares held in my account # ——- and mail the proceeds to me." I'd done it hundreds of times for many a Caboodle customer over the years. But it seemed to me that wasn't the worst part about holding so many mutual funds.

"What about paying taxes on any of the gains?" I asked Kitt.

"A mess. A huge fat mess. And she knew. Her accountant was in shock when she asked him to do her taxes. That's why she came in."

"To see Dr. Kitt, Portfolio Wellness Expert." Kitt laughed and went back to her desk.

Miss Eleanor Takes a Trip

For several months, Kitt and Mr. C had been talking about international investing. Everybody and his brother seemed to be starting regional funds for the Spice Islands or Special Situations in the Sub-continents, and Kitt was beginning to wonder if K&C was missing the boat, not starting an international mutual fund of its own.

"We just don't know enough about it," Mr. C said, whenever Kitt brought up the subject.

Then one day Miss Eleanor strode across the floors of our office, the same leather bag swinging from her wide shoulder, the same firm handshake across my desk, and asked, "Caboodle in?" before moving on to Kitt's desk. Kitt was in and stood to greet her large, cheerful aunt with a handshake of her own and a kiss on her aunt's ruddy cheek.

"Hi, Aunt Ellie. What's up?" asked Kitt, walking her to Mr. C's door.

"I've decided to take a trip, Missy. You and Carl can take care of things here, and my New York business is well in hand."

Mr. C. opened the door to his office and said, "Eleanor! What a pleasure to see you."

"Good morning, Carl. I was just telling Missy that I'm about to take a vacation. I've been planning this trip for years," she laughed.

Kitt laughed. "Which one are you taking?" She looked over at me and said, "Aunt Ellie has planned and canceled trips all over the world." She looked back at Miss Eleanor. "The one to Europe, or the one to Africa?"

"Yes. And the one to Britain. And to Australia and Singapore and China and Japan." She smiled broadly. "I'm taking them all. Going to bicycle in Britain and take a barge in France. Hike in the Himalayas. Backpack in Borneo. Cruise ship from Singapore to Hong Kong to Beijing, Korea, and Japan." She paused and smiled. "Remember all those brochures, Missy? I've booked them all."

Kitt laughed. "Don't tell me you're missing South and Central America."

"Of course not. I just haven't decided whether to take a boat down the Amazon or a cruise around the Horn." She reached into her capacious bag and pulled out a handful of colorful brochures. "Here," she said, handing them to Kitt. "You help me decide."

Mr. C looked worried. "Eleanor, how long will you be gone?"

"Oh, Carl, months and months. When you only take one vacation in your whole life, it takes a lot of time."

"But how will we get in touch with you?" he asked.

"Good heavens, Carl, you know we'll be in constant touch. From next Tuesday until sometime next Fall, I'll be Ellie@ Ell.com." Carl looked confused. She patted him on the shoulder. "Kitt will explain." She looked over at Kitt and me.

"I'll miss you all," she said. "But this is something I've wanted to do all my life. And now that things are going so well here and in New York, I can."

Kitt smiled, "They'll be buzzing in Backhoe. Wish I could go with you."

"I do, too, Missy. But you and Carl have to mind the store." Miss Eleanor put an arm around Kitt and said, "What souvenir would you like? You, too, Carl … and Caroline. Be thinking about what I can bring you back."

"How about checking out some of those international fund managers we've talked about, Aunt Ellie?" Kitt looked at Mr. C. "What do you think, Mr. C? She can see for herself if we should sponsor an international fund and, if so, what kind."

"Could you do that, Eleanor?" Mr. C asked.

"Of course. What else would I do with all my time? It's the main reason I'm going," she added. "We want to keep K&C on the cutting edge, don't we? Well, I figured I'd get my trip and due diligence in at the same time.

"So, teach him about E-Mail, Missy. He's going to need it."

So Miss Eleanor Kitt embarked on her once-in-her-lifetime vacation and Kitt began computer lessons with Mr. C.

Naturally, Mr. C had a Quotron machine on his desk. Everybody in the investment business does. You could get all kinds of information on it about customer accounts and K&C's daily research meetings, as well as the quotes on stock trades that it was named for.

But it wasn't hooked up to the Internet or anything like it, so Mr. C bought himself a little notebook computer. Kitt got one, too, so they could keep in touch with Miss Eleanor as she hiked and biked and

cruised around the world.

For Mr. C, this was a trying time. Everyday, he huddled over the instruction book and tried to puzzle out the little machine by himself. Everyday, his normal good humor would evaporate into frustrated fury and he would bark, "Kitt! I need your help here." She would get up and go into his office, closing the door to keep his anger from startling the other brokers.

But by the time Miss Eleanor had sent her third or fourth message, Mr. C was computer-literate and wired to the world. So proud of this achievement was he that he decided to subscribe to one of the many investment services.

"Might as well see what the customer can do without us," he explained to Kitt.

Poor Mr. C. He was dumbfounded by the amount of information available "without us!" He cried to Kitt one day, "I put this little diskette thing into my notebook and I can get information on every stock on the New York Stock Exchange, the American Stock Exchange, the NASDAQ National Market System, and the NASDAQ Small-Cap!" He almost spit out the last, he was so undone.

"Do you know that these people have found more than 200 variables for each stock so that I can screen by just about any criteria?" He dashed into his office and came out, carrying the little beige box. Clearing a place on Kitt's desk, he set it down and punched a couple of keys.

"Look! Just look at that! I asked for all stocks with price-earnings ratios below ten, price the same as book value, and look at the list? Got it just like that!" I couldn't tell whether he was happy or mad at this capability, but he was certainly excited.

Kitt got up and walked around her desk so that she could see the little screen. "Amazing," she said. "What else can it do?"

Mr. C pulled a book out of his suit coatpocket and read, "'Consensus earnings estimates for 4,000 stocks PLUS industry averages for comparisons, information on dividend reinvestment plans, nine different financial statements for each company.'" He looked up in wonder. "My God, Kitt, where have we been while this was going on?"

Kitt patted his shoulder. "How much did we pay for this service?" she asked. I think she was hoping that the cost was so enormous it would be beyond the financial reach of most customers.

"It's only $99 a year. Can you believe it? I had to join this group AAII to get it, but even if I hadn't joined, it would be only $150 a year," he groaned. "And they update it every quarter." He looked at Kitt in dismay.

"What in the name of Heaven does a customer need us for when they can get all this information on their own," he asked in a tone that suggested he was voicing the unthinkable.

"Now, Mr. C, you're panicking needlessly. *You know* that we've always believed in the Informed Customer. The more the customer knows about a company, the better off we all are. You know that's true, don't you?" Kitt looked at Mr. C earnestly. For a minute, I thought she'd tell him just to repeat after her, but she resisted. Instead, she gently took the instruction book out of his hand and began to flip through its pages. The Smile began its slow crawl across her face and lit up the darkness on Mr. C's.

"This is terrific. Look at this, Mr. C." She turned to the little computer and, referring to the book, tapped a few keys. Staring at the screen, she said, "Look at the company reports this thing generates." Turning to Mr. C, who looked a little less shattered now, she said, "You know, we could give subscriptions to this service to our really good customers, like Mona."

He looked at her uncomprehendingly. "What do you mean?"

"Well, it's not like we're giving away state secrets or anything. This is information that anyone can get from us if they ask for it, from the companies themselves, or from other sources. They could find a lot of this stuff out at the library, right?"

"Yes, I guess so."

"So now it's all organized in one place and easy to find." She lifted the little machine. "It's even easy to carry around. What a terrific thing!" Kitt laughed.

"I think we ought to give a seminar for our best clients on how to use their computers to access company research. And to find out the general consensus among analysts on earnings estimates. Good idea?"

Mr. C smiled, a little shakily. "Good idea," he agreed, and looked back down at the computer. "Good idea," he repeated, as he picked the little notebook up and carried it back to his office.

Kitt watched him go and then looked at me. "That stuff is amazing, Caroline. Let's find out what else we can do with this. Can we get stock quotes when we're away from the office? What else can our customers do without us?" She laughed a little uncertainly. "Are we stockbroker history yet?"

She picked up her phone. "I'm going to call 800 information and see if there's a listing for this AAII. What does that stand for anyway?"

"American Association of Individual Investors," I told her. "It's in Chicago."

"How did you know that?" she asked.

"I joined," I said. Kitt laughed again.

"When?"

"Back when you first told me that I should be an Informed Customer. Good group. Good information. And I've got their phone number. People can also join the National Association of Investors."

Kitt kept thumbing through the instruction book and pulling up information on her notebook screen. "I think this is great. But it's really for people who have a lot of time and interest in the stock market and in research analysis. There's a lot here that nobody would EVER have to know. In fact, if you have the Four-Season Portfolio Plan, you shouldn't have to spend a lot of time managing your portfolio. That's the whole point.

"I think this sort of stuff is good for the times you want to buy something new. Helps you screen out the losers. And it would be fun for the actively interested investor. But it's not for most of our customers. They just don't need to have this kind of research at hand. Or the time to use it."

"Or the interest," I added, thinking of my own sluggish attitude toward financial reports. To feel really guilty and totally inadequate, all I needed was access to 4000 companies' reports.

"Good for someone like Jack McWeedie. He's retired and treats his investment-managing like a hobby."

"Or for you when you want to work at home or check up on some of the analysts' ideas."

"Right. Why didn't *I* think of that?" Kitt said, picking up the phone to dial AAII.

After a lengthy conversation, Kitt hung up the phone and looked up at me. "I signed up," she said in a tone I can only describe as subdued.

"Okay. So what's wrong?" I asked.

"They told me that I can also sign up for a subscription to America Online. They have a forum for investors that gives all sorts of other stuff, information on financial software, articles from magazines, and a whole reference library. There was a lot more."

"Sounds great. So what's wrong?" I asked again.

"The reference library also gives information on discount brokers." Ah. No wonder she was subdued. She went on. "You know, Caroline, I was kidding before. But we brokers might really be history already."

"No way. Most people just don't have enough interest to do this themselves. And you do such a good job for people that they aren't going to leave you for some discount broker." I hoped I sounded more reassuring than I felt.

"Let's not mention that part to Mr. C, okay?" Kitt instructed.

"You got it. My lips are sealed," I said, trying to envision the unlikely circumstances under which I would even mouth the words "discount broker" in Mr. C's presence.

Meanwhile, true to her word, Miss Eleanor was seeing the world for herself and for us back at K&C, too. She E-mailed us almost daily, which thrilled Mr. C, because he was able to log on and tap in little answers of his own. He got so good at this that the slowest part of the process was his hunt-and-peck typing.

Using all her formidable zeal and curiosity, Miss Eleanor, as we all had expected, ferreted out interesting investment opportunities, fund managers, and stock markets everywhere she went. She told us, through cyberspace, that, while there were certain problems for Americans intent on investing internationally, it was something that everyone should still do.

Of course, Kitt and Mr. C agreed with her wholeheartedly. "That's why we have a Summer season in the Four Season Portfolio Plan," Kitt said to her computer one day, while reading her aunt's daily message.

"Things might be blooming everywhere in the world's garden, but it usually doesn't happen at the same time." She looked up at me, embarrassed to be caught talking to a screen. "We don't have to be sold on the

idea of international investing. We just want to know more about it. Right?"

"Right. Are you and Mr. C really thinking of starting an international mutual fund?"

"Well, if we did, we'd have to hire someone really great to manage it, and that's probably more expensive than sensible. More likely we'll just keep on doing what we're doing and recommend other approaches. That's what Aunt Ellie is going to decide for us. But with so many countries privatizing ..."

"Pardon me? Doing what?" I asked.

"Oh, sorry. Privatization means turning companies that were owned by the government over to individual investors. You know, like British Telecom a couple of years ago. Offering them in initial public offerings so that they become privately owned rather than government owned. There are some terrific, government-run companies that will be privatized over the next few years. Investors already know these companies and their services. They aren't baby companies. A lot of them are good, solid predictable adults.

"And lots of countries that were Communist have opened stock markets and are allowing people to buy pieces of local businesses, which gives us the opportunity to be part of their growth and prosperity."

"Or their wars, revolutions, and general chaos," I added, warily. Kitt laughed.

"True, true. But the opportunities are huge. And our U.S. market represents only one-third of all the money trading in capital markets around the world. International diversity can lower the overall risk to a portfolio, if you do it carefully."

"Just how could such stuff lower the risk to our portfolio?" I asked.

"Well, some years in the U.S. are horrible for our markets, but good internationally. Something good is almost always happening *somewhere.* There have been years in the past couple of decades when international investments have done MUCH better than our U.S. stocks and bonds."

"Okay. So we're back to Miss Eleanor out there checking out the best opportunities. What does she say today? What, in her view, are the problems, besides politics?"

Kitt looked at her computer screen again and said, "She lists them as currency fluctuation, less information on companies than what we get here, lack of regulation of securities markets, and lack of liquidity."

I got up from my chair and walked around my desk to Kitt's. Reading over her shoulder, I could almost hear Miss Eleanor's firm voice.

"In some of the emerging markets, insider trading is rampant and there is little liquidity."

"She means that there aren't many shares traded each day, so it's hard to buy and sell stocks when you want to," Kitt explained, looking up at me.

I nodded. I knew that already. "But what about this problem with currency fluctuation? How does that affect stock markets abroad?" I asked.

"Well, the other day, Aunt Ellie explained it this way: When she first got to France, and needed French currency, she got six French francs for each of her American dollars. Each franc was worth about 16 1/2 cents. The next time she went to the money changer, though, she got only five and a half French francs for each American dollar. Each franc was now worth about 18 cents."

"The dollar was weaker the second time she converted?"

"Right. So it bought fewer francs. She was a little peeved because that meant food and hotels and everything else was going to require more dollars, even though the prices in France hadn't actually gone up. Her hotel cost her 750 francs a night, or about $125, when she first got there. But when she changed more money and got fewer francs — 5 1/2 instead of six for each dollar — her hotel bill went up to a little over $136 a night. If the dollar gets weaker and she only gets five francs for each dollar, her 750 franc room will cost her $150. And you know how frugal Aunt Ellie is. If that happens, she'll be looking around for youth hostels."

"So how do these currency fluctuations affect our investments?"

"Well, let's say we got 6 francs for each dollar, and were buying shares in a French company. A share that cost 750 francs would be $125 a share when we bought it. When the conversion rate changed to the point where each dollar was worth 5 1/2 francs, that one share, without its price changing at all, would suddenly be worth a little over $136. And it could go up to $150 a share if the dollar got weaker and was worth only five francs. See?"

"Wow. So a weaker dollar is good for people who invest in international companies, but bad for people who travel."

"Looks that way. Of course, the reverse is true, too. And that's what worries Aunt Ellie about investing overseas."

"You mean that a strong dollar makes foreign stocks worth fewer dollars."

"Right. The franc could go back down in value and she might get, let's say, ten for each dollar. Her hotel room goes down to only $75 a night. But the price of that stock we might have bought goes down, too.

"Of course, that's true for any currency. The dollar getting weaker or buying fewer of whatever you're comparing it to — francs, British pounds, German deutschmarks, Japanese yen — means stock valued in that currency will translate to more U.S. dollars.

"And the dollar getting stronger against any of those currencies means the stock prices will translate into fewer U.S. dollars."

I sighed and said, "Every silver lining has a cloud."

"Right you are." We both read on.

"It's nearly impossible," wrote Miss Eleanor, "for a person in the U.S. to make sensible decisions by themselves when they want to buy individual stocks sold in a foreign country. It's hard to get the kind of information we're used to getting. In addition, the costs of buying and selling can be very high. End."

We looked at each other. "So what's the best thing to do?" I asked.

"Aunt Ellie is going to check everything out: American Depository Receipts — you know, those things called ADRs; multi-national U.S. companies; mutual funds that specialize in countries or geographic regions; international and global mutual funds. Those are the ways we can sensibly invest internationally. From what she says, it's dumb and expensive to try to do it directly."

"Is there a difference between international and global mutual funds?" I asked, "or was Aunt Ellie just getting repetitious?"

"That's what we've been using in the Four-Season Portfolio Plans up until now. The international funds can only invest in companies based in countries outside the United States. Global mutual funds can invest *anywhere*, including the U.S. Those managers buy stocks wherever they see the best opportunity."

"That sounds good to me."

"Well, not always. Sometimes we Americans already own enough U.S. stocks in other mutual funds or individually. We might already agree on which are the best opportunities and have those things in the portfolio already. Why overlap?"

"Good point."

As we mulled all this over, Miss Eleanor continued her travels, managing to keep up with her ambitious agenda of cycling and hiking even while touring the innards of local industry and interviewing local economists and politicians. Meanwhile, she summed up her growing body of knowledge with her daily E-mail messages.

"Impressed by Thisbie Limited. Good local and international business with expansion plans and decent management. We can buy its American Depository Receipts (ADRs) now selling on the New York Stock Exchange. They issue pretty good, almost U.S.-like financial reports."

ADRs are certificates that represent ownership in a foreign company's shares. The actual certificates are held by a U.S. bank, usually one with a lot of overseas business. But they can be bought and sold on our stock exchanges with U.S. dollars. If the company pays a dividend, it's also paid in U.S. dollars.

"In the Four Season Portfolio, why not cover the Summer Season by buying all ADRs?" I asked Kitt one day, soon after we bought some shares of Thisbie Limited for her aunt.

"Well, having *some* ADRs in the portfolio is fine. But only the largest companies actually issue them. We wouldn't be able to get ADRs for the small or even mid-sized companies that might be really terrific buys," Kitt said.

Miss Eleanor was particularly dazzled by the fact that some U.S. products were available in the most faraway corners of her circumnavigation. "I bought a Coke in Pango Pango," she wrote, "and listened to CDs of Dixieland jazz on the boat trip in Borneo. I see 'Made in the USA' signs and labels everywhere. Business is good for many companies that do business internationally, especially where you see good strong growth in the local economy."

Kitt began to look at multinational U.S. corporations, to see if they

would be appropriate Summer investments. Lots of companies were not only doing business abroad, but doing well at it. In fact, in some industries, the only real growth was coming from the international side of the business.

"If some of these companies pass through our screens and still look good, I'll buy us one or two. But I don't think multinational U.S. companies can really take the place of investing in a foreign country through a good mutual fund," Kitt told me one day over coffee when we were reviewing our own portfolio of stocks.

"Why not?" I asked.

"Well, first of all, say a company decides to do business in Australia, or Japan or Korea. They set up a facility or a distribution system and decide to make it work. This represents a big up-front cost and a long term commitment.

"What if the local economy falls apart for some reason? The mutual fund manager can get out of its investments there and move on to some more prosperous place, but the multinational company is committed to stay. So it's not as flexible an investment as an international mutual fund. Of course, some multinationals sell products easily all over the world.

"But another problem is that you're not only betting on the country's citizens being able to buy the product, you're betting on the product itself and whether it will be successful in foreign markets."

"So we should stay away from multinational U.S. companies for our Summer, international investing?"

"No. It may be the only way that some people will be comfortable with international investing. After all, with a company like Coke or Ford, you have no problem reading the reports or worrying about market liquidity or lack of regulation by the Securities and Exchange Commission. The foreign earnings are subject to currency fluctuation problems, but companies learn to handle them.

"But to really get all the goodies of international investing, like diversity in capital markets and growth that's often faster than we can find here at home, we should stick with the mutual funds, either international or global."

"Buy our own and rename it the Kitt & Caboodle International Stock Fund?"

"Not sure of that yet. We'll have to wait for Aunt Ellie to come home and help us decide."

Meantime, from Singapore, Miss Eleanor wrote: "Avoid country funds." These are the international or global mutual funds that can only invest in one country. "Too few good choices of companies to buy, simply too confining to be sensible. Unless I knew a country's politics and economy intimately, I wouldn't bet on a country fund. Expenses are high, too."

So we crossed the various country funds off our list of possible international investments.

Finally, Miss Eleanor came home. She was tanned and trim from the outdoor exercise, and she was full of excitement over her new international perspective. Her final judgment on whether K&C should start its own mutual fund?

"No. No need to buy our own. Or to hire a manager and build our own. There are so many good ones already out there, with low expenses and good management and low or no-loads." She paused to pass out some souvenirs she'd brought back for us, including a pink silk blouse for me from China.

Then, she went on, "We'd be foolish to try to compete with what already exists. Better to interview the managers of the ones with the strongest and most consistent performance over the past five years. After all, the world has been through a lot during that time. I want to see how these people have done when the dollar, and even whole countries, have been rising and falling.

"Let's check Morningstar's reports on the best international funds and go from there," she concluded.

"But, Aunt Ellie," said Kitt, "that's what we've been doing all along."

"True. But now I can ask these managers why they're more heavily committed to one region over another and understand their answers.

"And I've got some good ideas about ADRs and multinationals to include in our recommendations." Miss Eleanor looked at Mr. C and Kitt fondly, "I had a wonderful time. It was the vacation of a lifetime." Then she added, smiling at all of us benignly, "The one to have if you're having only one."

The Royal Georges Give Kitt Another Arrow for her Quiver

When Kitt first moved her things to the desk next to the two snooty Georges, they warmed up to her a little, accepting her questions with an air of noblesse oblige and giving out little tidbits of information like royalty throwing coins to the masses. She learned a lot about judging the quality of a stock by listening to those guys talk to their customers on the phone.

By then, we were having regular meetings together to go over our investment strategy, to talk about the companies whose stock we held, and to catch up on the latest gossip. One day, Kitt was more excited than usual. She started talking before I could close the door and spread out our papers in the Dining Room.

"One of George's customers asked him about inventory levels for a manufacturing company whose stock was going down today. And, you know what? He didn't know."

"Imagine. George *NOT* knowing something. What did he do?"

"Called the research analyst and blasted him for not giving out that information," Kitt said.

"Well, the analyst can't tell the sales people *everything*," I replied in defense of the unknown analyst. I'd defend Hitler against the Georges.

"Maybe not. But when a customer thinks it's important, it *must be*. As it happened, the analyst called the company and, sure enough, inventory levels *were* high because, he found out, the manufacturer is producing more than people are buying."

"Makes sense," I commented.

"Makes sense, but it's bad. That's why the stock has been going down lately."

This puzzled me. "But how do people know this kind of thing? How is some regular-person investor supposed to find out about inventory levels if the analysts don't even know?"

"Good question," Kitt said. "I asked the Georges that."

"I'm sure they care a lot about regular-person investors getting good information," I said with a snort.

"Well, they don't care at all about what regular-person investors

know, that's true. But they do like to show me how much *they* know."

I laughed. "So, did they have an answer?"

"Absolutely. Called it giving me 'another arrow for my quiver.' I'm going to call it the 'Outsider's Inside Information.'"

"Why?" I asked.

"Because that's what it is. Only it's legal. You know how we look at stock prices that are going up for no discernible reason and say to each other, 'Somebody knows something?'"

"Sure do. So?"

"Well, the Georges showed me how to look at the patterns those prices make and have a pretty fair idea of what might happen next. It's not infallible, but it's, well, another arrow in my quiver: Outsider's Inside Information."

"For Pete's sake! How long has this been going on?"

"Forever. Some people say this kind of analysis goes back to ancient times. Trying to figure out patterns in the way people buy and sell things. I don't know why more investors don't do this."

"Okay. How does it actually work?" Now I was really curious.

"Well, first it sounded like they were talking about escaping from prison or something: Breakouts, resistance, support. But when I looked at the price of National Brands over the past few months, I could see what they were talking about.

"It goes along with a theory of Charlie Dow, of Dow-Jones fame, back in the early part of this century. He noticed that once a stock started achieving higher highs and higher lows, or recording lower highs and lower lows, it kept moving in the same direction — up or down. Until something made it change direction. Sort of like the cows on the family farm."

Kitt smiled at the memory, while I waited for her to explain. "Once cows start going in a certain direction, they usually keep going in the same direction until something gets in the way and makes them stop.

"Same thing with a stock price. If it's on the way up, it keeps going up until it hits something. Then it can't seem to make it through a certain price to go higher. That's called the resistance level."

Kitt snatched a piece of paper off the top of her memo pad and took the pencil from behind her ear. She drew a line going in a northeast

direction, left to right.

"Dow, in what was called Dow Theory, identified three major trends in the way stock markets move. Individual stocks show the same trends. The 'primary' trend is the way things go over a long term." She ran her pencil across the width of the page to demonstrate.

"That's the direction that markets move for one to five years. Individual stocks, like National Brands, have primary trends, too." Kitt put little brackets around a portion of the line she'd drawn. "Then there's this 'secondary' or intermediate trend. That's the general direction of markets and individual stocks for, say, one to three months. And then," here she underlined a tiny area at the far right side of the page, "there are 'minor' or day-to-day moves in the markets, and in each stock.

"The idea here is that if you can spot a trend by looking at the price action over time, you can figure out if it's a good time to buy or to sell a particular stock — that is, determine whether it's on its way up or hitting the skids.

"Like Bancroft Communications, for example." She pulled out a piece of paper with lines across it. "George showed me this. It's the chart on Bancroft Communications ..."

"The what?" I interrupted.

"This thing is called a chart. The price for each day, high and low, is represented by a little bar, see?" She pointed out the little vertical lines across the page. "See how you can tell the direction over time?" I saw.

"The long-term 'primary' trend is up, see?" I saw that, too.

"But the intermediate trend is sideways, right?" I looked at the dates across the bottom of the page and saw that, sure enough, the price for the past couple of months hadn't moved above 14.

"And the daily trend, lately, has been down, see?" Kitt pointed to the little bars for the past week.

"Maybe a lot of people bought the stock at 14 and have been disappointed with it. For whatever reason, suddenly a lot of people are selling their stock. That's called 'supply.' Lots of supply at this price and not enough demand to get it through this resistance level. This is the price that stops this cow in its tracks.

"If it can break out of this resistance level, the theory is that it will keep going up. Now, when the cow, I mean the stock, changes direction,

it's called a 'reversal.' And down it goes. Lower highs and lower lows. Until it hits a level below which it's simply too cheap by anyone's measure. That's the stock's 'support level.' It should stop going down when it hits its support level."

Kitt pulled out the notes she'd made and referred to them. "George says that long-term support for Bancroft is at $8 a share. It hasn't fallen through 8 in price, no matter what, for two years. Intermediate support is at 11. If it falls through 11, it could plummet all the way to 8."

"So why," I asked, "is this the Outsider's Inside Information?"

"Remember our saying, 'Somebody knows something?'" Kitt asked.

"Yeah," I answered.

"As information about a stock spreads to the institutional investors — like George's guy, who asked about high inventory levels which turned out to be true — the volume of buying (or selling) picks up. All the cows gather together, momentum builds, and the stock price moves one way or another. You can see the volume here on George's chart for the past couple of months. Moving up." Kitt's finger ran along the bottom of the chart, where a little mountain range of lines marched across the page.

"Okay. These tall lines show a lot of volume at the same time the stock price was going down. *Meaning*?"

"Meaning it's not just some random selling, but a genuine disaffection for Bancroft. See, back here the price went up for a few months and the volume," her finger went back to the mountain range, "was high then, too."

"Okay. I think I'm getting this," I said. "You look at one of these charts to see the daily, the intermediate, and the long-term trends in a stock's price. Then you check the volume over the past couple of months to see if it's going up or is unusually high. Is that all?"

"No. Lots more stuff. Too much to use all the time. I mean, there are people who devote their days to this — so-called technical analysts who have and use all sorts of theories." Kitt set aside the paper she'd been writing on and pulled out another. "There are a couple of things we can use that are easy to find out and that should give us some good direction. At the very least, we can use this kind of information to confirm our decisions to buy or sell. It's not going to help us find out WHAT to do. But it will help us decide *WHEN* we want to do something."

I pulled out our investment portfolio file and opened it. "Okay. I sense a few more rules coming on. What are the Georges going to contribute to our expertise?"

"Well, first, let's find the trends: Look at the stock's chart for primary, secondary, and daily trends."

"No, FIRST, where can I find the chart?" I asked.

"We can buy a subscription to William O'Neill's *Datagraphs*," said Kitt. "They have charts on thousands of companies."

"So how expensive is that?"

"Well," she began, "I'm not sure. A lot of brokerage firms buy subscriptions so that brokers can send their company charts to customers who've asked.

"But individuals can subscribe, too. It probably doesn't cost a whole lot more than the commission on one or two stock trades. And if it saves us from making expensive mistakes, I'd say it's worth it. Wouldn't you?"

I agreed. "Okay. So after we've figured out the trends, what do we do next?"

"The Georges told me to look at a chart and write down everything I see." Kitt consulted the notes she'd jotted down during her audience with the Royals. "'Two-hundred day moving averages,'" she read aloud, then looked up at me. "Do we have a copy of *Investors' Business Daily* handy?"

I pulled the folded newspaper out from my wastebasket. "Here it is," I said, handing it to Kitt. She unfolded it and turned to the first section, laying it out flat on the top of her desk. Her finger began to trace a path across an illustration on the page.

"See?" She motioned me to look. "See this line? It's the 200-day moving average of the price of this company's stock." Kitt squinted at the name at the top of the small chart." This chart is for Demi-Tech Software."

She looked up and explained, "This newspaper highlights a different company each day. But you don't get individual charts for all companies in the newspaper. There wouldn't be room for that. The book of datagraphs gives you the individual charts." She pointed to the chart.

"Okay. See how the line is moving gradually upward?" I followed her finger and saw.

"They're taking 200 days of prices, dropping the last day and adding the latest one each day to see what the big picture is for price direction. Looking at 200 days of prices instead of just the past few days is supposed to smooth out the bumpiness, make the trends more visible.

"Here in this chart, they also show the 50 day moving average." I squinted at a barely visible line on the page.

"A magnifying glass would be helpful," I commented. Kitt laughed and continued with her explanation.

"See, this company's stock is trading above its 200 day moving average. According to George, you BUY a stock when it's trading ABOVE its 200 day moving average and SELL when it falls BELOW its 200 day moving average." I looked at the chart.

"That sounds a lot like buying high and selling low to me," I said. Kitt laughed.

"You're right. But remember, they trade a lot and like the upward momentum. I think the important thing about the 200 day moving average is the direction. If its direction is up, momentum is building. If it's down, interest in the stock is waning.

"It's interesting to look at a chart tracking the 200 day moving average for the markets, too. To get an idea about where all the cows are headed ... up or down."

"Where do we find that?"

"In the *Investors' Business Daily*." She flipped through and found the page with the Dow Jones Industrials, the NASDAQ Composite, and the Standard & Poor's 500. Then she flipped back to the highlighted stock chart.

"The other thing we should look for in here is the stock's relative strength. That means, how strong is this stock's price, how popular is it, how well has the price stood up in storms over the past twelve months compared to other stocks?

"You get all this information when a particular company is highlighted for the day.

"The instructions for reading the graphs are right under it," she said, pointing to a box headed "How To Read."

"But you can also find the relative strength in the daily stock columns of this newspaper."

Kitt flipped through the pages of *Investors'* until she came to the stock pages. Then she pointed out the first listing, which was for a company called AAR.

"See? Relative strength is the second number listed; it's 72 for this company's stock."

"Is that good or bad?" I still didn't get it.

"It explains here in the stock tables' How to Read box: 'Results are ranked 1 to 99. Stocks ranking below 70 indicate weaker or more laggard relative price performance.'" Kitt seemed pleased with her new tools. "Isn't this terrific?" she said.

"You can also find out what the strength of an industry is relative to the whole market; for example, how popular is the health care group when you compare it to all the 196 other groups that IBD follows?

"*Investors'* gives you that information in its stock tables on Mondays. See here?" Once again Kitt pointed to the "How to Read" box on the newspaper page.

"This explains that the groups are ranked by percentages, with the top 20% given an A, the top 40% a B, and so on."

"Why would I want to know *that*?" I asked. This technical analysis stuff was beginning to sound much too involved for my tastes.

"Well, if we're thinking of buying Demi-Tech stock and the industry is unpopular with the majority of investors, Demi-Tech will probably not go up in price, no matter how good a company it is. That's the theory anyway.

"But let's say the strength — or popularity — of Demi-Tech's group, which is software, is relatively good when compared to others.

"Then we look at how Demi-Tech's relative price strength compared to all other companies." Kitt quickly turned the pages of the *Investors' Business Daily* and found Demi-Tech's listing. She looked at the tiny print in triumph. "See?" she said, pointing to one of the headings.

"This is the relative strength of Demi-Tech: 78."

I was impressed. "That's really good information." Lucky thing that K&C subscribes to *Investors' Business Daily*. I asked, "What if I'm not here at the office but want to look up the relative strength of a company?"

Fat chance of that, but I thought I'd ask anyway, just in case. "Can I find this stuff in other newspapers?"

"No, I don't think so. This relative strength number is one that *Investors' Business Daily* comes up with, using their own computers, their own formulas, and their own database of 6000 companies. But it's pretty easy to find this paper on news stands. Libraries usually have it, too."

"Okay. So what are all the things we need to look at and what do they tell us about the company?"

"Strictly speaking, technical analysis doesn't tell us ANYTHING about the company. That's something we have to find out through fundamental analysis. Technical analysis only tells us about the company's price and the trends affecting it.

"I plan to use this information *only* when I BUY or SELL to confirm my TIMING, not whether the company is a good investment or not.

"The Georges do a lot of trading around of stocks in their portfolios," said Kitt, sniffing in disapproval. "If anybody wants to do that — OUTSIDE of the long term investments in the Four Season Portfolio — then this is a good way to keep them from making some really dumb decisions.

"And there's much more to technical analysis than just these few things. But for someone who's going to use the information for timing a purchase or a sale, these are the most basic things to look for: Trends (primary, secondary, and daily), 200 day moving averages, relative strength of company stock, and comparative strength within its industry group.

"And — for a small company — it's also nice to know if management owns any of the stock. I don't think we'd want to own a baby company if the management didn't want to own it, too," Kitt said. "On Thursdays, *Investors' Business Daily* publishes a column in its stock listings that tells what percentage of the stock is owned by management."

"How much is good? How *little* is bad?" I asked.

"George said anywhere from ten to twenty percent was a good number for small companies," Kitt replied.

So, maybe the Royal Georges *were* something more than royal pains in the, well, you know what I mean. They earned their keep with this one because it did keep me and Kitt from making some serious and expensive mistakes in the years that followed.

CHAPTER 11: SUMMING IT UP

Kitt and Caroline's Four Season Portfolio

After the first year, our joint portfolio was completely invested. We kept the Kicky Kola, had four other adult companies, two baby companies that have soared in good times and "have the glide path of a rock" (or so says Kitt) in bad times. I developed a strong stomach for their volatility.

We also owned some good, seasoned REITs, one high quality utility, a municipal bond fund, and an international mutual fund. We left all of these alone for several years, although Kitt insisted that we read all the company reports and research on everything. We did this once a quarter.

Early on, though, I started to do a lot of the research on my own. It was right after Kitt told me, offhandedly, one day, "You know, customers can read *Value Line* reports at the library."

"They can?" I asked. "But, isn't it sort of complicated for a ..." I searched for the right description. "... regular person to read? I mean, a non-investment-type?"

"Not at all!" said Kitt, standing up and walking over to the shelf of *Value Line* notebooks. Laying it on the table, she opened the notebook and lifted out a set of reports, bringing it back to my desk. "Look, I'll show you. It's really simple."

She smoothed out a report page with the name Bancroft COMM at the top left-hand side. "This is Bancroft Communications," she said. "You can see across the top here that it sells over-the-counter and that its symbol is "BCC." Her finger ran across the page. "These prices are a couple of weeks old, so I don't pay a lot of attention to them, but you can also see that it doesn't pay a dividend. Look, 'div'd yld Nil,' see?"

I saw. She pointed to a little box just under the name of the company.

"This is Value Line's value to me," she said. "They make judgments

on the stock that are usually pretty good."

The box read, "Timeliness," "Safety," and "Beta."

"They rank the company's stock on a scale of 1 to 5 for how well the price, according to their own research, will do the next twelve months relative to all the stocks they have in their survey."

"How many stocks is that?" I asked.

"About 1700. And the Safety ranking is important to me, too. It takes into account how much the price of the stock fluctuates and how strong the company is financially. I think we should stick with Safety rankings of 1 or 2. Those stocks aren't expected to go down as much as riskier ones if the market should fall apart."

"Sounds good to me," I agreed. (I hate it when the market dives.) "What's this beta thing?" I asked, referring to the next item in the box.

"Beta measures how sensitive the company's stock price is to changes in the stock market. Bancroft's beta is 1.60. This means that its stock can be expected to move 60% more than the market, both up and down. It's a small company, with not a lot of stock, so that's understandable."

"Okay. Tell me how to read the rest of this, please."

"Well, all of this is good stuff. But I'll just pick out the things that I look at first, that I consider to be the most important, okay?"

I nodded. She pointed to another box on the left-hand side of the page. "This tells some of the company's history. I like to know that. And this," her finger moved down the page, "this one headed 'Capital Structure' tells me how much debt the company is carrying as a percentage of its total capital."

I followed her finger. "'Less than 1%,'" I read. "Pretty good, huh?"

"Yup." Down the page the finger moved to "Current Position."

"Here's a quick little test to see how much working capital the company has. Ordinarily, you'd like to see about twice as much in assets as it has in liabilities."

"Okay. Bancroft passes that test, right?"

"Right. And you also find out how many shares are outstanding. This is a pretty small company, with only about 20 million shares of stock issued.

"Now this next box is really important to me," Kitt said. "See how it says 'Annual rates of change per share?'"

I squinted at the small print and nodded. "Well, here *Value Line* tells you both what has happened historically and what it predicts will happen in the future. So right here" — she pointed to the numbers next to "Earnings" — "we see at what rate the earnings are expected to grow." She lowered her voice and added, "I check these rates of growth against what our analysts are predicting. Sometimes our guys are wildly optimistic in their own recommendations."

"So this company's earnings are expected to grow at 24%, right?" I asked.

"Right. So what do you do with *that* number?" responded Kitt, answering a question with a question.

"I check it against the multiple. Then we can stick with our rule not to pay a higher price-earnings ratio than we're getting in growth."

"And a reasonable price for a company like this one with an estimated growth rate of 24% would be ..."

"... twenty four times the earnings per share. How do I find out what *that* is?"

"In this box ... See? It says, 'Earnings per share' and it has the actual earnings and the estimated ones for next year and the year after."

"So which one do I use?"

"Oh, I guess I'd use this year's for a small company with a volatile price. They've already reported three quarters here, so the year is almost over.

"In a minute, I'll show you how to find out if the earnings are easily predicted."

"Okay. So a fair price for this company with an estimated growth rate in earnings per share is 24 times .77?"

"Yes. That is" — she tapped on her little calculator — "about $18.50. Of course, remember that you have to watch a baby company carefully because it isn't as predictable as teens or adults. So those earnings may not come in as planned. But this gives you some good guidance."

Her finger moved up the page to the graph section. "This" — now she was pointing to the solid line that started in 1989 and ended in little dashes in 1994 — "is what *Value Line* calls the 'value line.'

"They multiply the company's cash flow by a number based on its anticipated earnings. It leads to this 'target price range.' I always glance at it to check its slope and also to see if the price is above or below the 'value line.'

"Remember, you take all of this stuff into account when you're doing your research before buying. There's an enormous amount of information here. The point is to see what it all adds up to.

"This big box of numbers shows the stock's history, plus estimates for some other things I like to know about a company," Kitt continued.

"Like what?" I asked, looking at the dizzying array.

"Well, all the way down here at the bottom, I check out '% earned on net worth.' This is the return on equity. It really says how well the company is doing with its shareholders' money. I think anything above 15% is pretty good."

"This is 15.5% now?" I asked.

"The whole year is estimated to be 15.5%. You can tell it's an estimate because it's in bold. And see this little notice?" She pointed to a tiny sentence embedded in the boxes of numbers. "This year and next year are, of course, just estimates at this point."

"Uh-huh. Do you pay attention to all these other numbers?"

"Sure. But these things I'm pointing out to you are the most important to me. If a company doesn't pass through this first screen, I don't bother with anything else.

"For example, I'll also check out rates of change in cash flow and book value, how the quarterly sales have gone — if there are any quarters that are always weak, for example — what the profit margin is, and if it's growing.

"But let's look at the rest of it for the Big Picture, okay?"

"Okay."

"Here in the 'Business box,' you can find out exactly what the company does. In just a few sentences, *Value Line* manages to get in all a company's divisions, how many employees it has, and in Bancroft 's case, the percentage of stock owned by a big mutual fund company. It also tells you how much stock the officers and directors own. Then you get the name of the company chairman, and the company's address and phone number, if you want to call for more information."

"A lot of stuff for just one paragraph."

"Sure is. The next box is really important, I think. And it's signed and

dated by the person who wrote it. This is a report of recent developments. It's updated every three months."

She pointed next at the little box in the lower right corner of the page. "Here's another *Value Line* Special: Value Line's own indexes of financial strength, price stability, price growth persistence, and earnings predictability. This is where we can see how reliable that earnings growth estimate is."

"It says '40,'" I noted. "Out of what?"

"Out of 100. So its predictability is on the low side. That makes sense for a baby company.

"And here is Value Line's 800 number, for people who want to subscribe instead of going to the library or asking a broker to supply them with these reports."

After that little study session, I began to look forward to reading up on each new company we considered for purchase. It's amazing how much information you can quickly get by doing this.

In addition, once a year, we'd go on an "investment retreat," which is really just an excuse to go somewhere interesting and check out other stock markets. The first year we could afford a retreat, we went to London; another year it was to Paris. I'm pushing for Singapore this year — there's a good airfare deal to get there and I like countries with clean public restrooms.

As for our portfolio's performance, there were a couple of bad quarters and even one bad year when everything we bought did terribly. Even though we had no plans to sell the Winter part — we just hold bonds until they mature — we priced them all each month, *in case* we wanted to sell them early. At times, when interest rates have been higher, our bond mutual fund has gone into the tank as well. Bond values go down then. But the fund continues to pay interest, which we continue to reinvest.

I got pretty nervous during those bad markets, but Kitt reassured me that the only way to win with investments over time was to hold them through thick and thin, so long as the reasons to own our stocks and bonds were still valid. Now, I hardly look at the portfolio at all between our quarterly reviews and annual retreats. It's so LIBERATING to know that this stuff is growing quietly in the dark without my help.

"Like mushrooms," Kitt said, smiling. She's so busy these days that it pleases her not to have to spend time managing our investments. But the more I learn, the more I want to do. You'd think I would be satisfied with our sensibly-invested and increasingly valuable portfolio, wouldn't you? I was, but I also wanted more.

The Four Season *Plus* Portfolio

As I said, these have been pretty good years for us here at K&C. Business has been terrific, with all these baby companies going public, teenage companies merging and acquiring, and adult companies coming up with new ideas and ways to grow.

Kitt and I have been overjoyed at the increasing value of our joint portfolio. At our quarterly meetings, we finger the statements lovingly, tap out the numbers on our calculators, and chortle to each other at the wonder of a successful investment philosophy. We've had some real turkeys, too, but we've agreed to shoot them quickly and replace them with something we hope will be better. The results are gratifying. We're rich. Or, at least, a lot richer.

"So, what happens next?" That's what I asked Kitt at one of our meetings a while ago.

"What do you mean?" she asked me back, sipping her expensive red wine, the color of good garnets, and gazing contentedly at the large plate in front of her. It held a small mountain of steamed vegetables on basmati rice. I know, I know. She (*and* I) could afford steak now but, better than steak (for Kitt), she could also get the attention of the chef wherever we went because of her newly acquired knowledge of good wine. And when she wanted steamed veggies and rice, she got them — no butter and no backtalk.

"I love our stocks," I said, spearing one of my sweet tiny scallops and popping it into my mouth. Mmmmmmm. "But there's nothing much to do now. All that information surrounds us every day. This technical analysis looks like a lot of" — I paused, searching for the right word — "… fun!"

"*And* … ?" Kitt asked.

"So what do we do now? We don't want to make any changes in our portfolio. The stocks are terrific ..."

"But you're itching to do something more. Right?"

"Well, yes. I'd like to use this technical timing device."

"I'm always on the lookout for good quality new names to add to our Four Season Portfolio. You know that." Through the basmati rice, Kitt's voice sounded slightly defensive.

"And you've done that well! Really well. But those things we buy are for all time — to hold forever — or we hope they will be, anyway. We never buy the things that go way up right away." I sensed from her sour look that I wasn't expressing myself well.

A small carrot slid off her fork, but she retrieved it. "And, have you noticed, most all those fast-rising stocks have also come *down* over time?"

Kitt was referring to some of the more exotic stocks with huge multiples that I had been intrigued by over the years. We'd always let her cooler head prevail and I'd been happy not to own those companies when bad times came and brought the prices down. Now I pressed on with my idea.

"Look, Kitt. We have this great portfolio that needs minimal attention. How about thinking of it as the body, or the bones, of our investments? We keep it healthy, maintain it over the years ..."

"And replace vital parts when they wear out ..." She smiled.

"Right. But also put part of it in the investment equivalent of, say, fancy clothes." I forked a few more scallops into my mouth and mulled over this concept for a minute. "You know, hot fashion items that you don't intend to wear forever."

I realized as I said it this that Kitt might not warm to the subject as much as I did because she bought clothes the way she bought stocks. Her closet held classics that were never totally *out of,* or for that matter, *in* fashion, but looked terrific on her. And once she bought something, she held onto it.

But I had her attention and she urged me to go on.

"Here's my idea. How about setting some money aside for a special portfolio, sort of a 'Four Season Plus?' We'd buy stocks that have short-term appeal, that we think will do well NOW but not forever." I was thinking of the early Basil stock and other specialty retailing types of companies.

"Sort of the miniskirts of the stock market," said Kitt, paraphrasing me.

"Right. We wouldn't mix those stocks into the Four Season Portfolio. They'd be strictly high fashion items."

"We'd have to keep a close watch on them," Kitt warned. "Most would probably be babies."

"I know. But with this technical analysis stuff and all the information that bombards us every day, I'd like to give it a try. How about you?"

The Kitt-smile spread across her face, brightening up the entire corner of the little restaurant. She lifted her glass of garnet-red and clicked it against my glass of mineral water. "I like it a lot!" she said. "Let's do it."

"How much should we use to get started?" I asked.

"How about 10% of the entire portfolio? If it grows, we'll trim back the excess and buy new names. If it shrinks, we'll ..."

"Worry about that when the time comes."

"Right. This is money we can afford to ... *lose*," she said, after first pausing, then nearly choking on The Word. She took a swig of wine to wash it down.

"So how do we decide what and how much to buy?" I asked.

"It's yours to decide," Kitt said. "You make the decisions for the 'Four Season Plus.' I leave it all up to you."

"To *me*?" Now it was my turn to choke.

"Of course. You're the fashion expert, not me. And you know technical analysis as well as I do. Put it together with some of the ideas our research people come up with and go for it."

So I did. We took some cash from a bond that had matured. Neither of us is excited about keeping too much in the Winter part of the portfolio. This withdrawal took its percentage down to about five. Combined with our Autumn holdings, which were our REITs and a couple of good quality utilities, we now had about 20% in the income side of the Four Season Portfolio. I'll grant you that neither of us is twenty-years-old any more, but here's the rule-of-thumb: the Winter segment of your total portfilio should be no *higher* a percentage than your age. If you want to take on the responsibility of babysitting, you can certainly have *less*.

Anyway, that's what Kitt and I think.

With the cash, I gave the orders to Kitt to buy things we both thought of as "special situations." Like a small financial services company that would benefit from an expected cut in interest rates. And a newly public coffee retailer that was expanding rapidly with spectacular same store sales growth. We also bought stock in a small technology company that was later bought out by a big technology company.

Each company whose stock we bought was in a strong industry with a good earnings-per-share ranking, according to the *Investors' Business Daily*. When we picked out a "special situation" company and confirmed its rankings, we would get its chart from the *Daily Graphs*. Often, we would see that the timing was right for purchase. If it wasn't, we'd go on to another idea.

Not all of our ideas worked. Some "special situations" were especially awful, like the software company that never got its new product to market, and the day care chain that swallowed other chains with borrowed money and then couldn't make its interest payments. The losses took painful bites out of our Four-Season Plus portfolio.

But high fashion is always risky — here today, gone tomorrow in some instances. I've learned to accept the risk and have happily added up the rewards, which have been pretty good.

Then and now, I make lists for everything or I forget something vital. It's not a sign of advancing age, mind you. I was this way when I was ten. Well, I got to worrying about what I would do if Kitt was out of town or in a coma or something.

So one day, she and I sat down and listed each of the steps that she advised people to take in the Four Season Portfolios so that I could manage alone if I had to.

Here is that list.

Kitt & Caboodle's Successful Investing Formula for the Four Season Portfolio

Step I

• First ask the following questions about your investment portfolio:

1. What is the purpose of the portfolio?
2. What is its time horizon?
3. How much money is available for investment?
4. How much risk in the portfolio is acceptable?
5. What are the tax considerations, if any?

Step II

• Review the investments that you currently own and figure out how they fit into the Four Season Portfolio.

• Check the percentages of growth stocks (shade trees) versus income producing investments (fruit trees). Is the percentage of income-producers higher than your age?

• What seasons are not covered, under-covered, or over-covered?

• List any alterations that need to be made to an existing portfolio (e.g., adding Spring and Summer growth stocks and international investments, and reducing Autumn and Winter investments.)

• Plan to make the alterations when the time is right; that is, when the price of a security is *fair* and technical analysis factors (relative strength, 200 day moving average, group strength, etc.) look favorable.

Step III

• Begin the search for new investments, or add to what you already own. Remember that you're going to have to maintain your portfolio by keeping up with the research on your investments and all the company reports.

• Keep the securities in your Four Season Portfolio to a number *you* can manage. How much initial and ongoing research can you realistically do?

Accept this as your personal responsibility. Kitt recommends owning between 7 and 15 stocks (bonds don't require as much maintenance), depending on the amount of time you can devote to portfolio management.

• To find new investments, consider local, publicly-owned companies you can visit easily and on which information is given in your local newspapers. Also consider companies whose products you use, or companies whose products you can research through people you know (e.g., doctors, computer systems analysts, auto mechanics, pharmacists). Ask the *customers* what the best company is in a product group.

• Diversify your choices across industry groups.

• Make a list of criteria to use in judging the quality of an investment so you can list the reasons you made THIS investment instead of another.

• Ask the same questions of *each* investment that you asked about the whole portfolio:

1. What is the purpose of this investment? (What Season does it fit? Is it for shade or for fruit?)
2. How long do I intend to hold this investment?
3. How much money do I have to spend for this investment?
4. How much risk am I taking with this investment? (Is it a baby, teen, or adult company?)
5. What are the tax considerations? (If its purpose is income, put it into a tax-deferred account, like the 401-K or IRA, if possible.)

Add the following questions for each new security you add to your Four Season Portfolio:

1. For growth stocks (shade trees): What is a FAIR price (P/E less than average growth rate in earnings per share)? Are technical factors favorable for purchase?
2. For income securities (fruit trees), see the utilities and REIT checklists.
3. For bonds: How have Standard & Poor's and Moody's, the two major bond-rating services, rated the bond's quality? What is the maturity date? What is the call protection?

Step IV

• Only after you've asked your questions, received satisfactory answers, and done favorable technical analysis, do you begin to buy. Just don't allow yourself to be paralyzed into inaction and lose out on the opportunity to afford retirement. *Get started now.*

See appendix beginning page 162 for investing worksheets and the complete list of commandments.

CHAPTER 12: TEACHING AS THE NEXT BIG STEP

Kitt Gets a Promotion

Though Missy Kitt had been working here at K&C for over eight years, she still looked like a stalk of corn from the fields of Backhoe, Nebraska: Reed-thin with silky red-blond hair. She may not have changed much in looks, but she'd definitely grown sleek and smart in investment know-how. So much so that Eleanor Kitt and Mr. C stood together in his office door a year or so ago and summoned her inside for one of their closed-door meetings. She told me later that they had offered her the position of "Director of Training."

"Is that something you'd like to do?" I asked, knowing as I asked it that she wouldn't be grinning like a lottery winner if it wasn't.

"It sure is."

I had to say it, though: "But, Kitt, Training isn't exactly a fast track to the top in the investment business. I mean, if you're going to stop being a broker after all your hard work, don't you think you'd have a lot more clout if you moved into the Corporate Finance Department? Or Mergers and Acquisitions? Practically ANYTHING else has higher visibility than Training."

It's sad but true. The investment business is, after all, in business to make money. Bringing companies public (Corporate Finance), and making deals with companies to merge them with others or to acquire new businesses (Mergers and Acquisitions) are big money-makers. That means that people who work in those departments get a lot more visibility for their work than someone training new brokers and retraining old ones.

"Who wants clout?" Kitt asked blankly. "I just want to get people to

do good quality business — brokers and customers alike."

She pulled the chair next to her desk up to mine and went on: "Aunt Eleanor and Mr. C have given me permission to start a school for investors. For customers, I'm going to set up regular classes in portfolio management, so that people can learn what they need to know in order to make good decisions."

"Wait a minute. K&C is going to pay for a school that teaches customers about investing? How did you get them to go for that?"

"Easy. Remember that story in the paper the other day about the guy who bought the exercise machine that simulates cross-country skiing?"

"No. What does that have to do with ..."

"He didn't know how to use it, fell off, and hurt himself. Instead of suing the company, which he seriously considered ..."

"Naturally. This is America."

"... he got the company's permission to do a training video. Now, people who buy the machine get the video, which shows them how to use the machine correctly. So they don't get hurt."

"Okay. I don't see anything unusual in that. A good idea, but what does it have to do with us?" I asked.

"The company making the exercise machine would rather train the customers in the *right* way to use it than be sued by people who get hurt using it the wrong way," Kitt said.

"Makes perfect sense."

"Yup. Aunt Ellie and Mr. C thought it made sense, too."

I was beginning to see her point. "K&C would rather train customers in the right way to invest than be sued by people who get hurt," I said.

"Naturally." Kitt smiled.

"So the job isn't to train brokers, but to train customers?" I asked.

"It's both. We'll have a school for brokers, too. But it'll be different than the usual boring training program they have to go through." She began to talk faster, a sure sign she was excited about this idea.

"We'll teach them the principles of Four Season investing. How to confirm the firm's research with technical analysis, Value Line, and Morningstar reports. How to read company reports and do some of the fundamental research themselves. How to understand what's right for the customers. How to explain it to them so they understand. Things like

that.

"K&C brokers will be the best-trained in the business. But, better yet, K&C *customers* will also be the best-trained in the business, too."

"That's a great idea, Kitt," I said. And it was. Is. She got me excited about it, too.

The first "semester" of the School for Investors was scheduled to start about a month after that conversation. For her first class, Kitt lined up some success storytellers. They'd give the attendees an idea of why they wanted to learn this stuff. I heard her on the phone with Mona ("Mom's Mums") Malloy.

"Most people don't have a clue about how or why a company would go public, Mona. Would you be able to talk about that for a few minutes?"

Apparently, the answer was yes, because Kitt continued, "If you have the time, I'll ask you to come back and talk at greater length later in the semester. Is that okay?" Again, yes.

"Oh, and do you think you could bring Emma? The 401-K plan is still a big mystery to a lot of employees and she's done real well with hers."

Mona must have agreed to that, too, because the Smile crawled onto Kitt's face and took up residence. She beamed it my way and gave me the thumb's-up sign. I quickly added the names of Mona and her daughter Emma to the list of First Night speakers.

When she hung up with Mona, Kitt thumbed through her not-so-little Rolodex file and pulled out another card.

"Who's that?" I asked.

"The chairman of the Board of the Back-to-Business Employment Agency — you know, my volunteer work. Their Endowment Fund is one of my accounts."

"I know. It's done really well, too, hasn't it?"

"Sure has. We were able to give Mrs. Kenilworth a raise and to also buy another copying machine." She pulled out another card from her file. "Let's call him for the first class, too ...

"And here are some other people who should talk to the class. Remember Mitch and Susie and their baby Joey?"

"Of course. Theirs was the first 'College Education Portfolio' that you

put together, wasn't it?" She nodded. "How's it doing, by the way?"

"Great. Gosh, it's hard to believe that Joey's ten now. Lately, we've been buying zero coupon treasuries with some of the assets because interest rates have gone up and there are some good deals out there."

"As I recall, that was a major part of the plan," I commented.

"Yup." Kitt looked proud. "And it's working out pretty well so far. Susie got a raise and decided to put it all into Joey's portfolio so the mutual fund part is pretty sizable. We liquidate shares when we want to buy the zeros." She leaned back in her chair and crossed her arms.

"Of course, grandparents have helped quite a bit, too. The neat thing is that the regular monthly contributions have bought the fund, whether its price is high or low. They get more shares when the price goes down and the account gets more value when the price goes up. That's the advantage of 'dollar-cost-averaging.'"

Kitt looked over at me and asked, "Susie and Mitch would be a really good addition to the first-night lineup of speakers, don't you think?"

"I sure do. I'll call them for you if you want," I said.

"Thanks," she said, handing me their card.

"And don't forget the McWeedies," I reminded Kitt. "I'll bet they'd love to come."

"Oh, the McWeedies!" Kitt laughed. "Try finding them at home. Or even in *this country*. They spend their time traveling from one Elderhostel to another. I think they're now somewhere in Eastern Europe, studying Medieval Art."

"Well, they couldn't have done it without you," I said.

Kitt considered this before saying, "They were good students."

At that moment, Mr. C walked out of his office. Lately, he had looked, well, different to me. I haven't been able to put my finger on just what it is, but he seems almost handsome in a craggy, country-squire kind of a way.

Eleanor Kitt appeared behind him, carrying her signature brown leather satchel-purse, and looking pretty handsome herself. Her normally straight hair had curls in it and, good heavens, she was wearing lipstick! At that moment, it dawned on me that the Kitts and the Caboodles might be working on a new and different kind of partnership.

As they walked by Kitt's desk, Mr. C asked, "How are the Investment

School plans going, Missy?"

Kitt pushed aside some papers on her desk and picked up the curriculum that she and I had set up for the first semester. She handed it to him. "Look at this, Mr. C. Tell me what you think."

"Will do." He folded the paper in half and tucked it into the inside pocket of his … was that a *new suit* he was wearing? From where I sat, it looked like one of those Italian silk numbers. Not Mafia Don or anything. Just very well-tailored and smart-looking. Hmmmmm.

We advertised the K&C School for Investors in the customers' monthly statements, in the newspaper, and on television. The response was phenomenal.

After a reporter interviewed Kitt about the School and did a story on how she was running a parallel school for brokers, we even got calls from other firms. (Seems there's now some sort of requirement for continuing education for brokers and this was an easy, inexpensive way for other companies' employees to satisfy the new rules.)

Other company employees like the classes because they're modeled after a regular college course, provide no buy/sell recommendations, use no specific company names, and are generic in nature. The purpose is to develop informed investors, not sell products or brokerage firms.

"It's Jeffersonian!" thundered Walter Goodale enthusiastically over the telephone. I had called to see if he would address the class on money management styles.

"No ads for your service, Walt," I stressed. "This class is generic — no brand names at all. This isn't a commercial for *any*thing or *any*body. Rules of the game." That's when he conjured up the name of Thomas Jefferson.

"Of course I'll do it. I believe in education. And it's Jeffersonian, so I couldn't possibly refuse. He's my hero."

I was interested. "How is it Jeffersonian?"

"Jefferson built the University of Virginia," said Walter, an enthusiastic UVA supporter and alumnus. "It's based on this belief: if you want the people to be an informed electorate, you have to educate them. Democracy can only exist, he said, if the voters understand the issues they're voting on."

Somehow Walter could say these things without sounding stuffy or pedantic. And he turned out to be a good speaker for the class, too. Now we use his Jefferson comment on the Investment School brochures.

Anyway, back to the curriculum list that Kitt gave Mr. C that day last year. He came back from lunch and sidled over to her desk with an odd, "we-need-to-talk" expression on his face. He stood there, clearing his throat, until she wound up her phone conversation.

"Hi, Mr. C," she said. "How was lunch?"

"Lunch?" he asked. "Good. Fine. Lunch was … Kitt." He cleared his throat again.

"Lunch was *Kitt*?" she asked, puzzled.

"No. Lunch was good. Kitt."

"Sir."

"I, uh, I …" He reached into his pocket, slid out the paper she'd handed him earlier, and laid it on her desk. "I like this lineup. Good stuff. Lots to learn here. Lots. For brokers *and* for customers."

"Thank you, sir."

"And for me." He looked uncomfortable. "I'd like to sign up. There's much in here that I never knew. This technical analysis stuff, for example. And I'd like to hear these young people talk about their investment plans," he said, pointing to several of the listed, first night speakers.

"You know, except for my driver Charles, I've never dealt with retail customers. Don't really know much about that part of the business. Do you think I could enroll?"

Kitt had to think about this for no more than a split-second, and then said, "Mr. C, I would be honored. And what a wonderful example it would set that even as experienced an investor as you is interested in continuing your education.

"You could introduce the program on the first night, telling about the Caboodles and their Keys to Successful Investing."

"You know, Kitt," Mr. C began, looking pleased with himself, "I'm finally writing my book about the family. I *could* talk about how they made money over the years."

"Great idea, sir. I'll put you down as our first speaker on the first night of the semester."

Well, all that's history now. The schools for both brokers and customers flourish. Kitt is running them from another building. She says it

gives them more credibility if they're completely separated from K&C. Several other firms help with the expenses, and the schools have grown to be pretty sizable.

I miss her, but she's doing what she does best and what may be most important: Helping ordinary people like me learn how to judge the quality of their investments and their investment advice.

WORKING YEARS PORTFOLIO (KITT/CAROLINE)

Name	# of shares	Purchase Date	Price	Cost	Reasons to own

enlarge 125% on letter size paper for easiest use

Retirement Portfolio (McWeedies)

Name	# of shares	Purchase Date	Price	Cost	Reasons to own

enlarge 125% on letter size paper for easiest use

Endowment Portfolio (The Agency)

Name	# of shares	Purchase Date	Price	Cost	Reasons to own

enlarge 125% on letter size paper for easiest use

Family Inheritance Portfolio (The Grandpa/the Progeny)

The Grandpa:

Name	# of shares	Purchase Date	Price	Cost	Reasons to own

In Trust for The Progeny:

Fund	Season/Reason	Manager	Amount/reinvested	Cost

enlarge 125% on letter size paper for easiest use

Mutual Fund Ownership for All Types of Portfolios

Fund	Season/Reason	Manager	Amount/reinvested	Cost

enlarge 125% on letter size paper for easiest use

KITT & CABOODLE'S 10 COMMANDMENTS OF INVESTING

1. Know why you own each security: for income (money you need now) or for growth (money you'll need later).

2. Write down the reasons you bought each security and sell only when those reasons are no longer valid.

3. Don't try to time the market: Diversify to lower your risk.

4. Know where a company is in its life story in order to understand its risk and reward potential.

5. Buy growth companies when the P/E is equal to or lower than the projected growth rate in earnings per share.

6. Know what can go wrong before investing in a company.

7. Read for ten to thirty extra minutes a day: *Wall Street Journal, New York Times Business section, Investors' Business Daily, Business Week, Forbes, Barron's, Fortune,* etc.

8. Always own some common stocks whose earnings are growing. That's the best way to maintain your purchasing power and to defend against inflation.

9. Income-producing investments (versus growth stock investments) should not be a higher percentage of the portfolio than your age.

10. If you find yourself NOT reading your investment mail, put it in a shoebox for safekeeping. Then schedule two hours every three months to read all recent company and research reports on your investments.

Calculating The P/E, Multiples and Growth Rate

- Price: $10
- Earnings per share (estimate for current year): .20
- Price divided by EPS (P/E): 50
- EPS (next year's estimate): .30
- P/E: 33
- EPS growth rate: 50%
- FAIR maximum P/E at this growth rate: 50

Checklist For Investing In High Quality Utilities

1. Dividend Payout Ratio
2. Regulatory Climate in State
3. Non-regulated Businesses
4. High or Low-cost Provider in Region
5. Customer Base

MUTUAL FUND CHECKLIST

1. Who is the manager?

2. How long has she/he been managing this fund?

3. What has been the fund's performance relative to the appropriate benchmark?

4. How well has this manager done compared to other managers of this kind of fund?

5. What does it cost to invest in this fund: load, 12-B-1 charge, management fees?

SPRING

When the Climate is Congenial for Growth

Growth investments:
own growth stocks

AUTUMN

When the Climate is Uncertain and Changeable

Income-producing:
cover the transitional season with stocks that pay good dividends but will still grow a little, like quality utilities and well-managed real estate trusts, as well as convertible bonds and convertible preferred stocks

SUMMER

When Things are Blooming and Booming in Many Parts of the World

Growth investments:
own international stocks so you can take advantage of different growth patterns

WINTER

When the Climate is Hostile to Growth

Income producing:
for a dormant economic climate, own fixed-income, high quality bonds like U.S. treasuries or triple-A corporate bonds

Hint: don't put more than your age into cold-weather investments

INDEX

ABOUT THE AUTHOR

In 1978, four years after earning a B.A. from the College of Notre Dame of MD, Susan Laubach went to work for a major New York Stock Exchange firm — Alex. Brown & Sons of Baltimore, MD. Entering the company's training program as a complete novice, she rose, over the next fifteen years, to become a retail stockbroker, a branch office manager, an institutional stock broker, a marketer of asset management services, and a trainer of other brokers. From this experience, she developed her notion of Four-Season Investing — simple concepts that made sense and money for her clients.

Laubach's idea of allocating investment money according to one's stage in life has also been enormously successful in her personal portfolio of stocks and bonds. She began with $5,000. Now, by following the same advice she gave her clients, her portfolio is valued at hundreds of times that amount. Four-Season Investing not only kept her financially on track, but enabled her to leave the business of buying and selling securities, to complete her graduate degrees (an M.Ed. and a Ph.D. from the University of Virginia), and to write this book.

In 1992, Laubach founded SBL Investment Education, where her clients have included several blue chip firms. She has been a guest lecturer at numerous prestigious universities. And she's been a featured speaker before such groups as the Young Presidents' Organization, the Society of Automotive Engineers, the Securities Industry Institute at the Wharton School, and the American Electronics Association.

She's also taken her investment advice to the general public. She hosted a weekly investment segment for cable television. And, since 1990, she's taught at the Chautauqua Institution in Chautauqua, New York (a 100 year-old summer program in Western New York). As she notes in the Introduction, she wrote this book partly because her Chautauqua students insisted that there was no such book on store shelves anywhere they looked.

Laubach, who's a Registered Investment Adviser, lives in Baltimore with her husband, Bob. She has five grown children and four grandchildren.

Susan Laubach is available for seminars and speaking engagements. For more information, contact SBL Investment Education at (410) 377-6810.